# A Big Surprise for Valentine's Day

Holidays with the Wongs, Book 4

Jackie Lau

First edition: February 2020

Print ISBN: 978-1-989610-43-5

Editor: Latoya C. Smith, LCS Literary Services

Cover Design: Flirtation Designs

# Prologue

VALENTINE'S DAY HAD NOT gone according to plan.

Instead, it had been Amber Wong's worst nightmare.

She returned to her apartment only half an hour after she'd left and shimmied out of her little black dress, then put on some fleece pajamas with penguins.

She glanced at the box of donuts *he* had given her. No sense wasting them. She pulled out the crème brûlée donut and took a big bite. The caramelized sugar on top was delicious, but she couldn't fully enjoy it.

Her phone rang.

She let it ring.

When it rang again two minutes later, she picked it up. She couldn't avoid this forever.

"You and Sebastian?" shouted her grandmother.

"Yes, Ah Ma. Did his parents call you?"

"Just ten minutes ago! Then I called Zach. He is at Cardinal's for a Valentine's dinner with Jo, and your parents are there, too."

So, everybody already knew.

Yep, her worst nightmare.

"But I don't understand," Ah Ma said. "Are you still together now? Should I be planning the wedding?"

"We were never really together."

"Aiyah, I do not understand young people these days. Tell me exactly what happened."

No way was Amber sharing any of those details.

"You are no fun," Ah Ma said in response to Amber's silence.

Amber sank onto the couch. Her head throbbed. She just wanted to curl up in a ball and watch baking shows.

"You better come for dinner on Sunday," Ah Ma said, "or I will drink two piña coladas."

Given Ah Ma's last experience with piña coladas—and that time, she'd only had one—this was a rather terrifying thought.

Amber laughed weakly. "I'll think about it."

"You want to get off the phone now and nurse your broken heart?"

"My heart isn't broken."

Ah Ma sniffed. "We will have a big talk when you come on Sunday."

"Maybe. If I come."

"You will be there!"

Amber finally got her grandmother off the phone and curled up in a ball like she wanted. She turned on the television, but she couldn't focus on the show.

Instead, she thought back to the day she'd encountered Sebastian for the first time in nine years...

# Chapter 1

*Several weeks earlier*

AMBER WONG WAS THE Queen of Bad Boyfriends.

She even had a cross-stitch that said so.

She took it out of her night table. There was a border of vines and flowers; the letters were blue and purple. *Queen of Bad Boyfriends.*

She'd stitched it in a fit of fury after her last break-up, almost a year ago now. Somehow she'd ended up dating another guy with a weird fetish for Asian women. You'd think she'd have figured out how to avoid these idiots, but no. She'd also managed to date a few cheaters and had more than her share of general douchebaggery. She'd even dated a guy who'd proclaimed, when he was drunk at a party, that women shouldn't have the right to run for public office. Or even vote.

Yet these men always seemed normal and well-adjusted to Amber when she first met them. She wasn't sure why her asshole detector was so bad, but it was.

Finally, at the age of twenty-five, she'd wised up. After finishing her *Queen of Bad Boyfriends* cross-stitch, she'd made another.

*Rule #1: No Dating.*

She'd hung it above her bed.

Amber had followed that rule scrupulously for the past eleven months, and she was proud of herself for that accomplishment.

However, there was one serious problem.

Sex.

She hadn't had sex in a year, and it was really starting to get to her. The toys in her night table saw quite a bit of action, but it wasn't the same as being with an actual human.

It was now January 5, and she'd made a New Year's resolution: have sex without dating.

She hadn't made a cross-stitch of that, however.

Back in university, Amber had had a fair bit of casual sex, but it was harder to meet people her age for a hook-up now. She could try an app, but she'd been putting that off, afraid she'd only end up swiping right on men who were total assholes.

At least she wouldn't be dating these assholes, just sleeping with them. Though it would be better to sleep with someone who was a half-decent person.

Amber rifled through her night table drawer. She tossed her collection of sex toys on her comforter, followed by her sexy lingerie, which hadn't seen action in a while. And she didn't expect that to change. Sexy lingerie was a relationship sort of thing, not something she'd wear with someone she was just going to fuck a few times.

*Ah, there it is!*

Finally, she'd managed to locate her squashed box of condoms. Since, with any luck, she'd be having sex in the next couple months, she figured she should start keeping them in her purse again, just in case.

She ripped three packets off the strip then noticed the numbers printed on the packets.

They'd expired.

She let out a rueful chuckle. She hadn't had sex in so long that her condoms had expired.

It didn't make sense, though. Condoms were good for a few years, weren't they? It had only been eleven months for her...though she'd stopped using condoms with that guy several months earlier.

Hmm. Maybe she had a newer box.

Amber searched through the rest of her night table and came up empty.

Alright. She needed to get condoms. Best to be prepared, and she was going to the bar with her friends tonight—perhaps she'd get lucky. Unlikely, but not impossible.

It was three o'clock and she wasn't meeting Gloria and Roxanne until seven. She'd run out to the grocery store, which had a pharmacy. Surely they'd stock condoms, and hopefully there would be discounted Christmas chocolate, too.

Condoms and chocolate. How wholesome.

Amber lived in Stratford, Ontario. Home of the Stratford Festival and the Ontario Pork Congress, as the sign said. It had about thirty thousand people, so it wasn't huge, but it was much bigger than the town where she'd grown up, Mosquito Bay, which had a population of less than two thousand.

Her apartment was nothing special, but fortunately, it was less than a ten-minute walk from the grocery store. She picked up a basket at the entrance and quickly located the Christmas chocolate. She was able to get cheap Santas and reindeer chocolate, plus some truffles. She also managed to find some candy cane ice cream for less than two bucks.

After that, she headed to the "family planning" section, feeling a little uncomfortable. Even though she was twenty-six and not at all ashamed of her love for sex, there was just something about buying condoms that made her cheeks turn bright red.

It was probably because of what happened the first time she'd tried to buy condoms.

She'd gone to the lone pharmacy in Mosquito Bay. Seventeen years old and ready to have sex with her first douchebag boyfriend. Thankfully, her father worked at the pharmacy in Ashton Corners, the next town over, and not this pharmacy. But as she was heading to the cashier, her grandmother came in, noticed the box in her hand, and screeched, "Aiyah! What are you doing?"

Ever since, Amber had hated buying condoms.

She looked left, then right.

No grandmothers or other family members. Excellent. Seeing as her grandmother didn't live in Stratford, it was unlikely, but you could never be too careful.

She knelt down and plucked a box of condoms off the shelf. When she stood up—

"Ow!" she exclaimed as she knocked into someone, who must have been reaching for something above her head.

"Sorry, I'm so sorry," said a low voice.

She rubbed her head as she turned around. The guy was kind of cute. A stocky East Asian man, her age or a little older, with short hair. Even his frown was appealing.

She had a split second to consider that he could help her with her New Year's resolution before she noticed the box of Magnums in his hand.

Amber couldn't help rolling her eyes.

She'd had two boyfriends who'd insisted they needed larger-than-average condoms, but honestly, they were both average size—which was fine. However, with the second boyfriend, the condom had slipped off, and she'd had to take the morning-after pill. After that, she'd insisted on normal condoms.

*But what if this man is actually...*

Well, whatever. Amber wasn't a size queen; she was the Queen of Bad Boyfriends. More likely, this guy had an inflated ego.

And then something truly horrifying came out of his mouth.

"Amber Wong? Is that you?"

Oh, God! This handsome guy with the box of Magnum condoms knew her!

She regarded him closely. There *was* something familiar about his features.

"Sebastian Lam?" she whispered.

He nodded.

The Lams had been good friends with her family when they were growing up. Sebastian was the same age as her brother Zach, and they'd been best friends.

Yes, someone who'd seen her play hopscotch and belt out tunes with a hairbrush as her microphone had now seen her put a box of condoms in her basket.

It seemed wrong.

"You've, uh, grown up," he said.

"Brilliant observation. I thought you were out west, doing your residency."

"I finished."

"And now you're working in Stratford?"

"Small town about twenty minutes from here. The doctor retired and I took over his practice, but I live in Stratford."

Sebastian had always been a good kid. His mother had bragged about him constantly, much to Amber's annoyance. He'd been a great student, excellent piano player, and then he'd gone to med school.

Holy shit, when had Mr. Perfect Son gotten so hot?

This was wrong.

Sebastian should not find Amber Wong so attractive.

He did some quick math. She'd be twenty-six now. He assured himself that there was nothing weird about a thirty-year-old man lusting after a twenty-six-year-old woman. Perfectly reasonable.

But this was Amber. Zach's little sister. The last time he'd seen her, she'd been in high school and he'd been in university. It was hard to reconcile the woman standing in front of him with the girl he remembered. He'd barely recognized her.

Her dark brown hair was in a low ponytail that curled over her shoulder, and her lips were pink and full and lickable. She was still petite, but she had curves that hadn't been there before. Very appealing curves.

"You have a romantic night planned?" He gestured to her basket, with the box of condoms and surplus of chocolate. Surely she'd tell him that she had a boyfriend, making her completely off-limits.

"You think Christmas chocolate and candy cane ice cream on January fifth means I'm planning a romantic night?"

He scratched the back of his neck. "I don't know. But...condoms."

"Useful things to have on hand. Mine expired."

He couldn't help chuckling.

"What about you?" she asked. "What are your condoms for?"

She said it casually, as though it didn't matter at all to her, but her gaze traveled over his body, and stupidly, he puffed out his chest.

He'd had a girlfriend in Vancouver. They'd been together for a few years; she was doing her residency, too, and they hardly saw each other.

Then he'd finished and wanted to move back to Ontario and she...hadn't. She was from Toronto, but she'd wanted to stay out there.

They'd broken up.

Frankly, he hadn't been as hurt as he'd expected, given they'd been together for so long.

That was a couple months ago now. He'd figured he wouldn't bother dating again for a while as he got his life settled in Ontario, but when he'd come to the grocery store for his weekly shop, he'd thought it wouldn't hurt to have condoms on hand.

And then he'd run into Amber.

Nothing would happen, but it was nice to have her looking at him appreciatively.

Sebastian had never gotten vast amounts of attention from women. A little, but not as much as, say, Zach. He was too serious, too quiet, occasionally gruff.

Normally, he'd be getting out of this awkward situation as fast as possible, but for some reason, he stayed. Not because she was pleasant to look at, but...

Okay, maybe that was the reason.

"Best to be prepared," he said with a grunt.

"But Magnums?" she said. "Puh-leeze."

He frowned. "What's wrong with my choice in condom?"

"Men who think they need those almost never do."

Well.

There were *so* many lines he could say in response.

"Is this from personal experience?" he asked.

"Yes. Condoms shouldn't be loose, you know."

"Don't worry, I'm aware of that. These fit...snugly."

Was he flirting with her?

Sebastian was not well-versed in the art of flirtation, but this might qualify as such, even if his tone of voice was all wrong.

"Right," she said skeptically.

That bothered him. Not because she assumed he was smaller than he actually was, but because she thought he was dumb enough to not know what kind of condom he needed.

He'd first had sex when he was twenty, and he'd purchased regular condoms. However, the condom had broken the second time, and after that, he'd invested in some larger ones.

He'd had no problems with broken condoms since then. Nor had any slipped off.

Amber tilted her head and stared at him, as though considering the size of his...member. Wondering if he was telling the truth.

She even licked her lips while looking at his crotch.

And then Sebastian did something so bold, he later couldn't believe it, though the fact that it didn't require him to speak probably made it easier.

He took the condoms out of her basket and dropped in a box of Magnums instead.

"That's presumptuous," she said.

He'd been paying careful attention to her body language. If he'd thought she would have been disgusted, he wouldn't have done it.

He managed a casual shrug. "I know."

"You should also know that I'm not interested in a relationship."

"Neither am I. I just got out of one."

"I have a tendency to date terrible men, so I'm taking a break from dating."

"But you miss sex, and you haven't had it in so long that your condoms expired."

"Yeah."

The silence. It was heavy.

This was not what he'd expected to happen when he'd arrived at the grocery store.

They continued to stand there as a woman walked down the aisle and picked up a bottle of shampoo, followed by some lube, before continuing past.

"That's a good idea." He grabbed a tube of lube and placed it in Amber's basket.

Her cheeks turned a delightful shade of pink, but he could tell she was enjoying this. Which was why he was still here, even though he'd known her since she was a small child.

But she was grown up now, and she could make her own decisions.

"You don't think this is a little weird?" she asked.

"It is," he admitted, but he was getting used to the idea. It didn't feel wrong the way it had when he'd first realized who she was.

She ran her hand over his bicep, which was covered in a gray sweatshirt. He wasn't wearing anything fancy, but her lips parted and she hummed in appreciation.

He definitely wanted to feel her hands on his skin.

He swallowed. "How about this. I'll give you my number, and if you decide you want to find out whether I actually need those condoms..." He glanced meaningfully at the box he'd put in her basket. "Send me a text, okay?"

That would give her some time to think about it—give them both some time to think about it—and leave the ball in her court.

He slid his hand over her neck, just above the neckline of her sweater, and to his satisfaction, she inhaled swiftly.

"You should know that I don't care about size," she said. "I'm not going to be impressed just because you're apparently bigger than average."

He shrugged. "I hear you."

"You sound like you don't believe me."

"Oh, I believe you. I also believe that I have the skills to impress you."

Why was he so cocky right now? It wasn't like him.

Most men probably thought they were better than average at sex, and it stood to reason that many of the men who thought that actually sucked.

But somehow, Sebastian was confident he could make Amber very happy in bed.

"You know," he said, "your ice cream's going to melt if you keep standing there with your mouth hanging open. You want my number before you head to the checkout?"

She held up her phone, and he entered in his number.

Then he strolled toward the fish counter, whistling.

It was only when he got there that he realized he didn't need any fish.

# Chapter 2

"LET ME GET THIS straight," Gloria said. "Your parents are good friends with his parents, you've known him your whole life, and now you're going to fuck him?"

Amber sighed and had a sip of her beer. "Maybe. I don't know."

They were at The Tempest, a bar they'd taken to frequenting recently. The walls were covered with posters of every production of The Tempest that the Stratford Festival had put on.

Amber worked in marketing for the Stratford Festival. It was basically her dream job.

When she was younger, she'd dreamed of being on stage herself. Unfortunately, she couldn't act. Or sing. Or dance. Or play an instrument. She had zero artistic talents whatsoever.

"Look," Gloria said, "I'm not going to tell you not to do this. You've had a long dry spell. But seriously think about it. I can't imagine sleeping with my parents' best friends' son. Dude is an ass."

"Sebastian isn't an ass," Amber said, "which puts him ahead of most of my boyfriends."

"Until today, you hadn't seen him in years. You don't know that, and you don't have a very good instinct for these things."

"That's a little harsh," Roxanne piped up from the corner, speaking for the first time in five minutes.

Roxanne and Gloria were Amber's closest friends, and in the mostly-white city of Stratford, the three of them stood out.

Roxanne, a Black woman with a quiet temperament, was an incredible dancer—she worked part-time at a dance studio. She lived in Waterloo, forty minutes away, where she and Amber had gone to university, but came to Stratford on a regular basis and crashed on Amber's couch.

Gloria—louder and brasher—was third-generation Chinese-Canadian, like Amber, though she wasn't biracial. She currently had a pixie cut and was wearing black fishnets with a short black skirt, black sweater, and bold jewelry. She worked as a costume designer and was a wizard with a sewing machine.

Yeah, Amber definitely couldn't approach the talents of her friends, but that was okay.

"He doesn't have to be the greatest guy ever," Amber said. "I'm just going to sleep with him, not fall in love."

Truth be told, she figured it would be pretty hard for her to fall in love now, after all her shitty experiences. One day, she'd try again, but at present, her "no dating" rule was firmly in place.

A white dude in a trucker hat approached their table. It was clear who his eyes were on: Gloria. "You Japanese or Chinese?"

"I'm Canadian, you punk," Gloria said.

"Hey. All I did was ask you a question. Can I buy you a drink?"

"Nah, I got a girlfriend."

The guy smirked.

"And she owns a boxing gym, so I'd watch it if I were you."

The guy eventually returned to his table of dude-bros at the front of the bar.

"Bet he has some kind of strange Asian fetish." Gloria shook her head. "Probably thought I'd be sweet and submissive."

"Pretty sure you're right," Amber agreed.

"I love being able to truthfully say that my girlfriend owns a boxing gym. I'll keep saying it even after we break up."

Roxanne's eyebrows drew together. "Are you having problems with Syd?"

"Nah, but you never know. We're coming up to the six-month mark, and my relationships never last more than six months." Gloria gestured to Amber's phone. "You got a picture of this guy of yours?"

"He's not *my* guy."

Gloria made a dismissive gesture.

It took Amber a minute, but she found Sebastian's profile on Facebook. There was a photo of him—unsmiling—with trees and a tent in the background.

Gloria looked at it in horror.

"What?" Amber said. "He's decent looking, isn't he?"

"Tent," Gloria whispered. "Camping. He likes...camping."

Roxanne shook with laughter.

Amber laughed, too. Gloria enjoyed playing up her hatred of camping.

Amber turned her gaze back to Sebastian's profile picture, and suddenly, she imagined that mouth on her neck, where he'd touched her earlier.

It would be crazy to date him. The thought of her parents and his parents finding out they were together...that was the definition of hell. But they wouldn't actually be together, and Amber was sure Sebastian was sensible enough not to say anything.

In fact, sleeping with Sebastian really was sensible. Safer than sleeping with a stranger.

And sure, Amber didn't care about size, but she couldn't help being intrigued, plus she hadn't felt chemistry like that with a guy in a while. She'd spent a disturbing amount of time thinking about Sebastian since she'd returned from the grocery store that afternoon, and he was certainly a better prospect then any of the guys in this bar.

Amid all posters of The Tempest on the bar's walls, there was a poster that was out of place: the Justin Bieber one.

Stratford was, after all, his hometown.

So Amber did whatever she, Gloria, or Roxanne did when they had a dilemma and were sitting around The Tempest with their drinks.

She lifted her beer toward the poster and said, "Justin Bieber, what should I do?"

But she was already pretty sure of what she wanted.

On Sunday evenings, Amber sometimes went to Mosquito Bay to have dinner with her family, but this morning, she'd decided that she wasn't up for the hour-long drive and would prefer to spend the time doing other things.

Her family, however, decided to take an impromptu road trip to visit her.

At eleven o'clock that morning, her parents and grandparents barreled into her apartment.

Amber's mother, Rosemary, was white, and her father, Stuart, was Chinese. Her paternal grandparents lived in Mosquito Bay, a few streets over from their son.

"Happy New Year!" Ah Ma said, giving Amber a hug. "You do anything exciting to celebrate?"

"Just hung out at the bar with my friends."

"Did you dance with any guys?" Ah Ma gyrated her hips as best she could.

"No."

"Did you kiss anyone?"

"No."

"Did you get drunk?"

"Not very."

"Amber, I am disappointed in you! You are supposed to be living an exciting life!"

Amber had been the wild child in high school, to the exasperation of her family. Her brother Greg, eight years older than her, was the polar opposite of wild, which had set certain expectations for the rest of them. Nick's wild years had come later, once he was in Toronto. Frankly,

Amber didn't think she'd been all that different from Zach in high school, but she was the baby of the family—and the only girl—and anything she did seemed to worry her family more. As a result, they'd received a censored version of her exploits in university, as well as her relationships.

Now that she had a full-time job and lived on her own, they would sometimes ask her to tell them exciting stories, then be disappointed that she'd never been whisked away for a romantic weekend by a star hockey player—or whatever they expected.

In fact, they'd become rather obsessed with her lack of love life lately.

"I got you a scarf on Amazon." Ah Yeh, her grandfather, held up a piece of cream fabric. "It is a Hamlet scarf."

Since she'd started working at the Stratford Festival, Ah Yeh had begun buying Shakespeare-related things for Amber. As a Christmas present this year, he'd gotten her salt and pepper shakers with Shakespeare's face on them.

"Thanks, Ah Yeh." Amber wasn't sure if a scarf with quotes from a Shakespearian tragedy would go with any of her outfits, but she'd make a point of wearing it at a family gathering this year.

"I brought you some beef stew and butter tarts." Mom handed her two containers.

"I made you coconut lemon squares!" Ah Ma raised her hand in the air.

"No, you did not," Dad said. "If you'd tried to bake, you would have burned down the house."

"Wah, I am not that bad at baking!"

"She didn't start a fire the last time she tried to make them," Ah Yeh said, "but she used salt instead of sugar. They were terrible."

"Then why don't you make them?" Ah Ma retorted.

"I did! You don't remember?"

"Hmph. You probably ate them all and didn't leave any for your poor wife."

"You have a bad memory."

Her grandparents continued to bicker until they were all sitting around Amber's small dining room table with cups of tea.

An hour and a half later, her family was out the door, and Amber collapsed onto her couch. She enjoyed seeing her family, but she often felt like she needed a relaxing afternoon at the spa afterward. Alas, that wasn't in her budget. However, she could think of another activity that was very good for stress relief.

Sebastian checked his phone. Still no text messages.

Well, of course there weren't any. If he'd gotten a text, his phone would have vibrated to tell him so, and his phone had never been more than a foot away from him for the past twenty hours.

It was Sunday afternoon. Sebastian had made himself fried rice for lunch, and now he was relaxing with a mug of tea and a book on his recliner.

At least, he was supposed to be relaxing, but he kept checking his damn phone every five minutes.

Even when he wasn't looking at his phone, he was having trouble concentrating on his book. He kept thinking about sliding his hands through Amber's hair. Maybe pulling it a little, if she was into that. He would ask her what she liked.

But it had been almost a day, and he was worried she wouldn't contact him.

And that was fair. They'd known each other since childhood, and it was a little awkward, he understood. He wouldn't blame her if she decided against it.

Still, he was hoping...

Sebastian nearly jumped out of his chair when his phone finally vibrated.

He couldn't help feeling disappointed when he saw that it was his sister. He was about to put his phone back on the table, but then it vibrated again.

*Hi, it's Amber. I'm interested. Are you free this afternoon?*

# Chapter 3

Amber considered changing into a more revealing top. But she didn't want to make a big deal of this, so she left her sweater on, though she changed from her frayed pajama pants into a pair of jeans.

Her phone rang. Sebastian was here.

Her heart beat a little quickly as she buzzed him in. A minute later, he was standing inside her door, his large frame making her apartment seem small.

Yeah, she definitely still wanted him. It hadn't just been a quirk of her brain that had found him attractive yesterday.

But although Amber had had a lot of sex before, and a decent amount of casual sex, it had never seemed quite as awkward as it did now.

"Hi," he said.

"Uh, hi." She paused and glanced toward the bedroom. "Let's lay down a few ground rules. This is just sex, and under no circumstances will our parents find out about it."

"Agreed."

This seemed so transactional.

Shit, was it going to be too weird?

He scratched his chin. "Is there anything in particular you like or don't like? Any boundaries I shouldn't cross?"

She wouldn't wear sexy lingerie for him, but she didn't think he'd expect that anyway.

"Off the top of my head, no," she said. "I'll let you know if anything comes up. Today, I think I'd like it rough."

"Okay."

"Just don't leave any marks that I can't easily cover with my clothes."

He padded over to her couch and sat down. "Come here."

Hesitantly, she walked over and sat on his lap, straddling him.

He grabbed her ass firmly in his large hands, and she gasped. This was still a bit weird, but in a good way.

He lifted up the bottom of her sweater and the T-shirt underneath and slowly dragged them up her body. She was acutely aware of the fabric sliding over her skin. He tossed her clothes on the floor, then placed his hand at the clasp of her bra. When she nodded, he threw that on the floor, too.

His hands were all over her skin now, as were his lips and teeth and tongue, and the man was *good* with his mouth.

As he was feasting on her, he kept one hand on her ass, the other arm on her back with his hand gripping her hair.

"You okay?" he murmured, lifting his head to her ear.

"Yeah. Just keep going."

An infuriating smirk touched his lips. He dove back down and latched onto her nipple, biting it lightly before soothing it with his tongue.

She grabbed the bottom of his long-sleeved shirt. He separated from her just long enough to pull it over his head, and then he was lavishing attention on her other breast.

She pressed herself against him, enjoying the incredible feel of his warm skin against hers. It had been so long. Too long. She'd craved this sort of contact, and...*oh*.

There were multiple layers of clothing in the way and she couldn't see it yet, but yes, she had the sense that he'd been telling the truth about needing Magnum condoms.

She reached between them and undid his jeans with shaking hands. Why was she shaking? It wasn't like she hadn't done this many times before. He helped her slide off his jeans and boxers, and she rolled to the side to get a better look.

He was long and thick, definitely a little bigger than anyone she'd been with before.

And he would put that inside her.

She squirmed, practically grinding herself against the couch.

She had a momentary fear that he was too big and it wouldn't fit, but she pushed that aside. A ridiculous thought. Of course it would fit.

Sebastian unzipped her jeans and thrust his hand into her panties. She inhaled swiftly as his finger slid over her entrance.

She watched his hand, inside her jeans, moving in and out of her, and then she looked at his body, all gloriously naked. She couldn't decide what she wanted to look at more.

The fact that this was Sebastian, whom she'd known her whole life, somehow made it filthier, in a very good way.

He pulled off her jeans and underwear then returned to fingering her, getting a better angle than before. She squirmed against him in pleasure-filled agony and reached for his cock.

"Please," she said.

It was the first word either of them had uttered in a long time, and he didn't say anything in response, just grabbed a condom out of his jeans and put it on. She positioned herself on all fours in front of him. When he rubbed the tip of his erection over her instead of thrusting inside, she pushed back against him in frustration.

His chuckle, as he began to push into her, was low and—

"Oh. You really are big," she whispered. "Go slow."

The tip of him still inside her, he leaned over and kissed the side of her neck. His body surrounded hers, and it felt good, but when he started to push in deeper...

"Ow."

Dammit, why wasn't her body co-operating? She hadn't had sex in eleven months, and she needed this. She craved it.

Or maybe that was the problem: she wasn't used to this.

Sebastian pulled out. "Where's the lube I tossed in your basket yesterday?"

"Let's go to the bedroom."

She jumped off the couch and walked toward her bedroom, glancing back to check that he was following her. He was, his ample erection encased in latex, bobbing between his legs. She threw herself onto the bed and opened her night table. The lube was right on top.

She got down on her hands and knees again, heard Sebastian slick himself with lube, and then a lubed finger circled her entrance.

The tip of his cock was next.

"Ow."

She couldn't believe this. It wasn't going to fit.

"Keep going," she said, not ready to give up.

"Are you sure?"

"Yes." She took a deep breath. "I know it'll feel good soon."

He pushed in a little more but had trouble getting in any farther.

When he pulled out, she rolled onto her back, mortified. She'd envisioned a hot, quick, and sweaty encounter, but it wasn't going according to plan.

"We don't have to do *that* today. I don't mind." Sebastian glanced over at her bedside table, the drawer still open. "You have a nice collection of toys in here. We could try one?"

Now she was even more embarrassed. He could see her sex toys. She had seven—did he find that excessive? His expression betrayed no judgment, though.

She grabbed her dildo, which was about the size of a small penis, rather than Sebastian's monster cock. It was clear glass with pink ribs. He took it from her hand and peered at it curiously, as though he'd never seen anything like it.

He set it on the comforter. "I'll use it in just a minute."

He climbed on top of her and slid a finger into her again. She wasn't as wet as she'd been a few minutes ago, but she got a little wetter as he continued to fuck her with his finger, then added a second.

And then he kissed her.

She realized, with a jolt, that though they'd been all over each other, this was the first time he'd kissed her on the lips. He tasted faintly of coffee, with a hint of pine, an unexpected but appealing taste. She coaxed his lips open and slipped her tongue into his mouth, and he hissed. He was still turned on, despite everything.

He continued to finger-bang her with gusto. When he stopped suddenly, she whimpered against his mouth.

He sat up and held the dildo to her lips. As she took it into her mouth, desire flashed in his eyes.

"I want to see your lips around my cock," he said.

"Now?"

"No, maybe next time."

*Next time?* She couldn't think that far ahead.

He crawled backward down her body, took the toy that she'd slicked with saliva, and pushed it inside her. Her body accepted it without difficulty.

"You feel okay?" he asked.

She nodded.

He pumped the toy in and out of her, his gaze riveted on her crotch.

Something about letting a man use a toy on her—during their first time together—was oddly intimate.

Sebastian lay down on his stomach and licked her as he continued to fuck her with the dildo. She squirmed against his face, and when he swiped his tongue over her clit, she grabbed the comforter in her hands and cried out for him.

He crawled up her body, a self-satisfied grin on his face, and kissed her.

She wanted more.

"Let's try again." She bent her legs and spread them as wide as she could.

He removed the toy, and then his stiff cock was at her entrance. This time, he watched her face as he pushed inside. When her breathing hitched, he stopped, but when she nodded quickly again, he kept going, until he was fully seated inside her.

"Good girl," he murmured, and it made her stupidly pleased.

She could feel her body stretching to accommodate him, and there was the tiniest bit of pain as he pumped in and out of her, but it was good this time. He pushed his hands through her hair and tugged her head back, just a bit, allowing him access to her neck. She moaned.

"Yes, that's right," he whispered. "You're taking it. Taking it hard." He pounded even deeper inside her, and she cried out.

He wrapped his mouth around her left nipple and sucked before he pulled out and arranged her on all fours—like the first time they'd tried this—and thrust into her again. As he fucked her, he stroked her clit, sending her over the edge once more in a spiral of pleasure.

Through the haze, she heard him grunt, low and long.

After he pulled out, he held her against his chest, anchoring her to the world as her breaths gradually slowed.

"Is this okay?" Sebastian asked, tightening his arm around Amber.

This was what he'd usually do after sex, but maybe it was against the rules. Too affectionate, perhaps? He didn't want to do anything she wasn't comfortable with.

"Yes." She cuddled up to him. "I miss physical contact."

She didn't care that it was *him*; she just wanted a warm body in her bed. And that was fine with Sebastian, it truly was.

"Has that ever happened before?" she asked. "The not-fitting business, I mean."

"My second girlfriend was a virgin. It took three separate tries before we managed it."

"I'm far from a virgin, though."

She sounded worried that he'd been disappointed in her performance, but nothing could be further from the truth. It had felt amazing to slide inside her...but also to taste her and watch as the toy moved in and out of her body.

"I would like to do it again." He figured it was best to be straightforward about this. "Not today. Another time. If you're interested."

When she nodded, warmth spread inside him. He pulled her closer and planted kisses up and down her neck.

Yes, he would enjoy this arrangement. It was exactly what he needed after getting out of a long relationship. He'd just have to make sure there was *lots* of foreplay, as well as lube. He'd treat her well and ensure she always had a good time. It would be mutually beneficial.

Okay, that didn't sound sexy at all, but it was true.

They lay in contented silence for a few minutes. Then he sat up and started looking for his clothes.

"They're in the living room," Amber said.

He was about to head to the living room, but then he noticed the piece of fabric hanging above her bed. Cross-stitching, he thought it was called.

*Rule #1: No Dating*, it read.

She really was serious about this no-dating business.

Which was fine.

His gaze dropped to the top of the bedside table, where the dildo was sitting. It was wet from her moisture, and God, that was nearly enough to make him hard again.

Next to the dildo, there was a collection of crochet birds. He picked up the peacock. Though it was small, it was extraordinarily detailed.

"Did you make these?" he asked.

"Yeah."

"Did you buy a pattern?"

"Nah, just made it up myself."

He looked at the peacock, then back at Amber. "You're very talented."

She rolled her eyes, and dammit, that pissed him off.

"No, really," he said. "You are."

She shrugged. "Nothing like how you can play piano."

"But I can't do this."

She didn't say anything, but she smiled up at him, and he ran his hand down her back.

Yes, he would enjoy this arrangement very much.

# Chapter 4

"Wait a second." Gloria put down her latte. "You're telling me he was ginormous, but he was actually good in bed? In my experience, the guys with the biggest dicks are also the ones who have no idea how to use it. They think being big is all they need to do."

"Yeah, he was good," Amber said. "And when it didn't fit the first time—"

"*It didn't fit?*"

"Just a little louder." Amber looked around the coffee shop. "I'm not sure everyone heard you."

Gloria laughed. "Sorry. I'm imagining—"

"Please don't imagine."

"Alright, alright."

"Anyway, when it didn't fit, he wasn't frustrated, just gave me an orgasm before trying again." Amber tried not to get lost in her memories of Sunday. Had that orgasm been particularly good because she'd had nothing but self-induced orgasms in almost a year?

"So you're going to keep seeing him?" Gloria asked.

"Yeah."

"And you're not falling in love with him?"

"Definitely not. This is the ideal set-up. Just what I need." Amber paused. "How long should I wait before I text him again?"

Gloria gave her a look, then sipped her latte.

"Seriously, it's nothing more than sex." Though Amber couldn't help recalling how close to him she'd felt when he slid the dildo inside her.

Physically close, that was all.

They'd fucked, nothing more.

Well, they'd snuggled for ten minutes, too, but it didn't mean anything. He'd left right after that.

"I've been sex-deprived for so long," Amber said. "I need to make up for lost time."

"I'd wait another couple days."

After she got out of the shower the next evening, Amber walked into her bedroom and picked up the crochet parrot and peacock sitting on her night table.

Sebastian had said she was talented, and she'd brushed him off. Besides, what did he know about this stuff? But secretly, she'd been rather pleased.

Cross-stitching and crocheting were things she did to keep her hands busy, often while watching baking shows. Things she did just for herself that other people almost never saw.

In fact, with her last boyfriend, she'd always dumped her crochet animals into her dresser before he came over, afraid he'd laugh at her.

But it hadn't occurred to her to do that with Sebastian—maybe because she was so out-of-practice with this sex business—and he'd actually liked them.

She had nothing on Gloria's or Roxanne's talents, but it was nice that he'd been kind.

Her gaze traveled down to the knob of the top drawer of her night table, and she couldn't help the little moan that escaped her lips.

He'd been kind and filthy and enthusiastic, in his own serious way.

Amber couldn't wait any longer. She sent him a text.

Friday evening, Amber was doing a little cleaning as she waited for Sebastian.

When her parents called, she answered the phone with a sigh, hoping this would be quick, but that was probably too much to ask.

"Hi, Amber," Mom said. "You're coming over for dinner on Sunday, right?"

"I'll be there, don't worry."

"What are you doing tonight?"

Well, obviously Amber wasn't going to tell the truth about that. "Oh, not much. Just staying home and tidying up. Watching TV."

"Staying home on a Friday? That doesn't sound like you."

It wasn't super unusual for Amber to be home on Friday night, even if her family assumed otherwise.

She sneezed as she dusted the small table in the corner of the living room.

"Are you sick?" Mom asked.

"Uh, yeah." Amber hoped that would put an end to any questions about her Friday night plans.

But saying she was sick only led to other questions, of course.

"What are your symptoms?" Mom demanded. "Do you need to talk to your father? He's the pharmacist, after all. Actually, I have some chicken soup in the freezer. Why don't I bring it over right now—"

"Mom, that's really not necessary."

It was unlikely her mother heard, however, as there was some banging on the other end of the phone, and a moment later, she heard a different voice.

Ugh, it was one of those days when she had to talk to every member of her family. Her paternal grandparents were at her parents' place all the time.

"You are sick?" Ah Ma asked. "Did you go to bed with your hair wet?"

"No, Ah Ma."

"Hmm, you don't sound sick to me."

Now that Amber had said she was sick, she couldn't admit she was lying. She let out a weak cough and made her voice a little fainter. "It's not too bad. I'm sure I'll be fine by Sunday."

Dammit, Sebastian would be here any moment. She needed to get off the phone.

"Hi, Amber." That was her dad. "Sorry you're feeling under the weather."

"Thanks." She managed a fake sniffle.

"Make sure you get lots of rest."

"I know."

"And don't listen to anything your grandmother says about wet hair. It's bullshit."

Amber wasn't surprised to hear yelling in the background.

Her mom came back on a minute later. "Are you sure you don't want me to bring soup?"

"Positive. I can order soup here if I need some."

"But it's not the same as your mother's chicken noodle soup."

"Of course not, but it's an hour drive. It's not necessary, and I'm really not that sick."

"You sound pretty sick to me."

What? Her grandmother had said just the opposite two minutes ago. Maybe Amber was playing it up a bit too much now.

She glanced at the clock. "I need to get going. I have, uh, something on the stove."

"Of course. I'll call you in an hour to see how you're doing."

"Mom!"

"Just kidding. Go to bed early and have a good night's sleep. Talk to you tomorrow. Oh, wait. Your grandfather wants to talk to you."

"I—"

"Hi, Amber," Ah Yeh said. "I hope you feel better soon. I just sent you an email with some books about Shakespeare that I thought might interest you."

"Okay, thank you, Ah Yeh. I'll look at them tomorrow." She let out a weird-sounding fake cough. "See you on Sunday."

And finally, she was off the phone.

Thank God.

·♥·♥·♥·♥·♥·

Sebastian arrived a few minutes later, and this time, there were no awkward hellos. This time, Amber threw herself at him the instant he walked through the door, and he responded by growling and kissing her back...then lifting her up and carrying her straight to the bedroom, where, after lots of foreplay and lube, he slid into her from behind without any problems and fucked her hard until they both cried out.

It was unfair, really, that he got to be Mr. Perfect Son *and* be so good at sex.

Afterward, she snuggled up to him again, relishing the luxury of having a man in her bed. Sebastian was about five-ten, and solid. Not solid muscle, no, but she loved his strength.

"The other day," she said, "I was masturbating, and I thought of you the whole time."

His eyes darkened. "Did you use your toys?"

She nodded.

"Good girl." He paused. "Do you like when I say that? If not, I won't do it again."

"I like it." It reminded her of the fact that she was younger than him, that he'd known her when she was just a girl—and that seemed delightfully wrong.

*But it's not wrong now,* she told herself.

"I considered sexting you," she said.

"Yeah?" The corner of his mouth quirked up. His smiles were often lopsided, and for some reason, she liked that.

"But I didn't know if you'd be into it."

"I'd be into it." His voice was rough.

"Ooh, you know what would be fun? We could have a code word that either of us can use when we want to sext. Then the other person can reply yes or no, if it's not a good time."

"Bubble tea," he suggested.

"No, that's confusing because you might actually want bubble tea one day. Unless you hate it."

"Of course not. I miss it, actually. It's one of the things I miss about being in the Vancouver area, where I could get any Asian food or drink I wanted."

"But you came back."

"I came back."

His arm was around her, and he was absently—or perhaps not-so-absently—running his hand over her side.

"You didn't want to live in Ashton Corners, though?" she asked.

That was his hometown, fifteen minutes from Mosquito Bay.

"Ha," he said. "Have you met my parents?"

"You think they'd be surprising you with visits every day?"

"Absolutely."

She could imagine it, yeah.

"You wanted to be close but not too close," she said.

"Exactly."

"That's what I wanted, too. Close enough that I can easily visit, but far enough that I won't run into them at the pharmacy when I'm reaching for a box of condoms. Far enough that they won't barge in with chicken soup the instant they learn I'm sick." She paused. "My mom called right before you came. She was surprised I wasn't going out tonight, and since I didn't want tell her about my plans with you, I said I wasn't feeling well. And then Dad, Ah Ma, and Ah Yeh all insisted on talking to me."

Sebastian laughed. "My parents bought the house next door to them."

"Your parents *what*?"

"The house next door was for sale, so they bought it last year. They did a bit of work on it and *heavily* implied that they wanted me to move there when I was done my residency and work at a practice in one of the neighboring towns."

"By 'heavily implied,' you mean they talked about it constantly during every phone conversation."

"That's exactly what I mean."

What a horrifying thought. Amber was speechless.

Living next door to her parents? She didn't know how Zach lived in Mosquito Bay—and he, at least, was a ten-minute walk away from their childhood home. Much as they liked to interfere, she couldn't imagine her parents buying the house next door and expecting her or her siblings to live there.

But Sebastian's parents? Yeah, she could see it.

Apparently he wasn't enough of a pushover to go along with their wishes. Good.

"Are they still hoping you'll change your mind?" she asked.

"Yes, but they don't talk about it much anymore. I think they know they'll have to sell the house. They did some work on it, and they should be able to make a little money, even though the real estate market in Ashton Corners isn't exactly hot."

Amber started laughing. "I still can't believe it. I mean, I can, but it's just so ridiculous. They bought the house next door!"

"Sure, sure," he muttered. "Laugh at my misery."

She slid her hand up his chest. "We still need to come up with a code word or phrase. How about 'house next door'?"

"Amber…"

"Fine, fine."

"Sonata." Sebastian had chosen a music word, of course.

"Okay," she said. "When one of us texts 'sonata' to the other person, that person can reply 'yes' or 'no,' no questions asked."

They were quiet for a moment, and Amber simply let herself luxuriate in his presence. She loved sex, but she'd always loved the after-sex cuddle and conversation, too, and she was glad she could have that with him.

Eventually, she began stroking her hand over his leg. First his shin, but then she moved higher...and inward.

"Thank God you caught me reaching for a box of condoms," she murmured as she grasped his cock.

He growled and pulled her on top of him, so she was sitting on his face, and circled his tongue over her entrance.

And then they had lots more fun.

That Sunday, after recovering from her pretend illness, Amber went to dinner at her parents' house and imagined, with fresh horror, living next to her family. Her horror magnified when Ah Ma tried to get everyone to tell her what sixty-nine was.

Yep, no way in hell would her family *ever* learn about her and Sebastian.

Besides, if her family found out, his family would know, too...and they wouldn't approve of her. They'd thought she was too wild ever since she'd given their daughter a "dirty" book in high school. And telling them that she and

Sebastian weren't *actually* together wouldn't make things better.

Yes, sleeping with him was worth it, but they needed to be careful.

# Chapter 5

Sebastian was in the car with Amber, which was, in all honesty, not somewhere he'd expected to find himself. But when he'd texted to ask if Wednesday would work, she'd suggested he come over at six so they could do something first. As in, before sex.

"Where are we going?" he asked again as they drove east out of Stratford, passing through the village of Shakespeare.

"Oh, you'll see," she said airily.

He grunted. He liked to know what he was doing in advance.

Amber was wearing work clothes: gray dress pants, a checkered vest, and a white collared shirt. He'd never seen her dressed up like this before, and it made him even more desperate to get her naked. Except, even though this "relationship" was supposed to be casual sex, they were heading out of town.

"Zach has a girlfriend," Amber said. "Jo MacGregor. She was a few years above you in high school."

The name was familiar, but Sebastian didn't remember this woman.

And the mention of Zach caused a pang of discomfort.

They'd been close friends when they were younger, but they'd drifted apart when they went to different universities, though they'd still seen each other from time to time. Then Sebastian had gone out west for med school, and he hadn't really kept in touch with anyone in Ontario except his family.

He'd planned to text Zach once he was settled in Stratford.

But then he'd started seeing Amber.

"How's Zach doing?" he asked.

"You haven't spoken to him since you got back?"

"No. I feel a little awkward about it. It'll be weird to talk to him without saying anything about you and me. I'll call him, though. Just not yet."

"He's doing well," Amber said. "Teaching science at our old high school—you knew that, right?"

"Yeah."

"Jo is the first girlfriend he's had since his broken engagement. I'm glad he's moved on."

Sebastian nodded, and they slid into silence.

Where on earth were they going? They'd been in the car for thirty minutes now.

Finally, they pulled up to a plaza in Waterloo, near the universities. When they got out of the car, Amber grabbed his hand and led him to the right, then seemed to realize they were holding hands and let go.

He felt a momentary disappointment but pushed it aside.

And then he saw the bubble tea shop.

He wasn't accustomed to bursts of joy, but there it was.

It was partly because he was going to have bubble tea for the first time since he'd moved across the country, but also because Amber had gone out of her way to take him here.

Maybe it was more the second than the first; he didn't examine it too closely.

Before she reached for the door handle, she turned back to look at him.

"Should I not have taken you here?" she asked. "You mentioned missing bubble tea, and I thought...well. I hadn't had it in a while either, and there's a pan-Asian restaurant in Stratford that serves bubble tea, but it's not very good. My friend Roxanne lives in Waterloo and we come here sometimes—it's my favorite tea shop in Waterloo. Of course, there aren't nearly as many here as in Toronto or Vancouver, but this one is good, trust me—"

Sebastian jerked her away from the door, cupped her cheeks in his hands, and kissed her. She squeaked in surprise, but she started kissing him back almost immediately, her arms winding around his neck. One of her hands slid through his hair, and that felt good, too, but not as good as her lips and her tongue stroking his.

"Woo-hoo!" someone shouted.

Amber and Sebastian jumped back from each other. There were a couple teenagers standing nearby. Were those kids even old enough to be in university? Were they drunk, despite it being before seven on a Wednesday evening?

Sebastian took Amber's hand and pulled her inside.

"Sorry for kissing you in public," he mumbled.

Her cheeks were a little pink. Perhaps she was a touch embarrassed—or maybe that flush was just from his kissing skills—but she didn't seem too bothered.

He'd kissed her because he'd wanted her to stop babbling...

And because he'd simply wanted to kiss her.

They ordered their bubble tea, and he handed over a twenty-dollar bill before Amber could get her wallet out.

"Hey!" she said. "You're not allowed to pay."

"Why not?"

"This isn't a date. We're friends. I don't want you to get the wrong impression."

"I'm not. We took your car, so I'm paying."

"Fine, fine," she muttered with an exaggerated frown.

They took a seat by the window, next to some kids wearing University of Waterloo sweatshirts. Geez, he felt old. The people around them were all in their late teens and early twenties, and he was the grumpy old guy.

Though he was sitting with the prettiest woman in the tea shop.

"I can't believe you got banana milk tea." She gestured to his cup.

He took a sip and got a tapioca pearl and mango jelly along with the milk tea. "Why not? Banana is delicious."

"Ugh. You were probably one of those kids who liked getting sick so you could have that stupid banana-flavored medicine."

"Amoxicillin."

"Yeah. That."

"I wouldn't say I liked being sick, but if I was, I always hoped I'd have to take it."

She shook her head, as though he was hopeless, but in an affectionate way. "I only like cooked banana. Banana bread, for example, is delicious. But that? Not for me."

Amber had ordered taro milk tea with tapioca, and she looked cute with her lips wrapped around that straw.

She also looked cute in that vest. He'd suddenly developed a massive thing for vests.

"If I remember correctly," he said, "my parents told me you work at the Stratford Festival."

"Yeah. In marketing."

"Do you like it?"

"It's perfect for me. I always wanted to work in the arts, but not actually performing. I had a few jobs in Toronto after I graduated."

"I didn't know you lived in Toronto."

"For a couple years. Did whatever work I could get—which wasn't always related to my degree. A lot of temp stuff."

"Did you like Toronto?" he asked.

"I enjoyed being there, but I didn't want to live there permanently. I guess after growing up in a small town, the big city was a bit overwhelming. My current life suits me just fine."

He was glad she had a career she enjoyed. Not everyone managed that—especially not by the time they were twenty-six. He liked his, but it was stressful at times, especially now that he was running his own practice.

It had been barely a month, though. It would get easier.

But he'd had to give bad news to a patient today, and that was always tough.

Yeah, he'd really needed this time away from home tonight. He felt awkward thanking Amber for it, but he reached over and gave her hand a quick squeeze.

She looked a little baffled.

His phone rang and he checked the display. "It's my mom."

"It's okay, you can get it," Amber said.

He picked up the phone. Probably best to answer, as she might keep calling otherwise.

"Hi, Mom," he said. "I'm kind of busy right now, so if you could keep this short, that would be good."

"What are you doing? Are you still at work?"

"I'm out with a friend."

"Which friend?"

"Not someone you know."

Across the table, Amber laughed, apparently amused that she was a "friend," even though she'd called him that just ten minutes before.

"Come over for dinner tomorrow," Mom said. "I will make your favorite, but I need you to take down the Christmas lights."

"Surely that's not a rush. Christmas was three weeks ago. Can I come on the weekend instead? Another couple days won't hurt."

His mother clucked her tongue. "Tomorrow, okay?"

"Okay. But why can't you or Dad take down the Christmas lights?"

"Your father could break his neck. He is getting old. Do you want that on your conscience?"

"No, of course not."

"Tell me who this friend is. I heard a woman's laughter. Is this friend a girl? Do you already have a new girlfriend?"

"That's just someone sitting at the next table."

"Why are the tables so close together? What kind of place are you at?"

"A bubble tea shop," he said.

"In Stratford?"

"In Waterloo."

"Why did you drive all the way to Waterloo on a work night?" she demanded.

"Look, Mom, I really have to go. I'll see you tomorrow."

He set down his phone and massaged his temples.

"You are such a pushover," Amber said.

He shrugged. "After years of being out of the province and only visiting once a year, I'm now less than an hour away. I feel like I owe them. I can let myself be pushed around a bit, but I draw the line at moving in next door."

"Why did you go so far away for med school?"

"I didn't get into any med schools in Ontario."

She nodded. "I know it's competitive."

He was glad he'd gone to the other side of the country—it was nice to experience something different. But now he was back home. Not Ashton Corners, but close.

He'd always intended to work in a small town. Some towns found themselves without a doctor when theirs retired. At least in southern Ontario, the towns weren't too isolated, but still.

Amber gestured at his toque, which was sitting on the table. "Is it strange experiencing winter again after living in Vancouver?"

"I kind of missed winter, actually."

"You freak of nature. You like winter?"

"I like having four seasons, though I'm not a big fan of hot summer days. Winter is better."

"Ugh, what is wrong with you?" she teased.

When they finished their bubble tea, it was well after seven.

"So, uh." He scratched the back of his neck. "Time to head back to Stratford?"

"Let's grab something to eat in Waterloo first. There's a good Taiwanese fried chicken place near here, or there's a sandwich bar that does pretty decent banh mi. Which would you like?"

"Fried chicken."

"I was hoping you'd say that, but I figured I'd better give you an option." She grinned.

He had a large piece of crispy fried chicken for dinner. Hardly healthy, but that was okay. He would eat well tomorrow.

Even though this was *not* a date, as she'd made clear, he couldn't help wanting to put his hand on her knee. In fact, he couldn't help feeling like they were teenagers on a first date, unable to afford anything fancier than fast food.

*It's just lust*, he told himself.

Lust and friendship. Yes, that's what it was.

She popped another piece of popcorn chicken in her mouth, and he shifted in his seat. Goddammit, what was it about seeing Amber Wong in work clothes, eating fried chicken, that made his pants so tight?

"What's wrong?" she asked.

"Why do you think something's wrong?"

"You're glaring at me."

"I'm not glaring at you."

"You are." She gave him a look.

"Fine. Maybe I was. You're just so..." He gestured toward her helplessly.

"I'm what?"

"Cute," he said accusingly. "In a grown-up way, of course. The way you eat popcorn chicken seductively...it's cute."

"I'm not trying to be seductive! I'm just eating."

"Sure, sure."

Maybe she wasn't trying, but he seemed to find everything she did seductive.

When they got back to Stratford, it was nine o'clock. He appreciated that she'd taken him out for bubble tea, and they'd had a good time together, but his body had been ready to jump her three hours ago.

Though he'd been itching to remove that vest for hours, now that he had the opportunity, he decided to leave it on.

Sebastian carried her to the bedroom and set her down on the edge of the bed. He sat down behind her, his legs outside of hers, and kissed up and down the side of her neck as his hands roamed over her chest—on top of her clothing. For now.

When she writhed against his cock, he unzipped her pants, then slid his hand inside her panties, finding her warm and wet for him. He brushed his fingers against her clit; she inhaled sharply.

He captured her mouth in his. Unlike their last kiss—in front of a bubble tea shop, of all places—this one was private.

"You taste like fried chicken and banana," she murmured.

"Sounds delicious." He pressed his erection against her back. "I think you like bananas after all, don't you?"

It was horribly lame, but she burst into gratifying laughter.

And now, it was time for her to make other noises.

He got off the bed and knelt before her. He pulled off her pants, then the pink underwear underneath.

As he set his mouth to her, he looked up. She was still wearing her white shirt and that sexy vest, like she was a professional career woman, but her head was tipped back, her lips parted in pleasure, and it was so hot.

He finger-fucked her roughly as he rolled his tongue over her clit, savoring her taste. He took his cues from her sounds. They got louder, and he worked her with his fingers and mouth until she was shrieking out and shaking for him.

When she had come down from her orgasm, he stood up and shifted her up the bed so her head was on the pillow. Then he finally unbuttoned her vest and tossed it on the floor, along with her shirt and bra. Now he had full access to her breasts. He cupped one in his hand and plucked the nipple with his fingers before setting his mouth to it.

She squirmed.

He slid two fingers inside of her as he continued to suck her breast.

She squirmed some more.

"Yeah, that's good," he said. "You like my fingers in your pussy, don't you?"

He glanced up to see her nod, and then he kissed her mouth, giving and taking as much as he could before sliding down her body so his mouth could join his hand.

His cock was rock hard, but he wanted to focus on her. Wanted to get her ready to take him.

Amber came again. She was quieter this time, but she shook and gripped the comforter.

"Sebastian," she groaned. "Please."

"Tell me what you want."

"You know what I want."

"Amber..." he said sternly.

"I want your cock."

Fuck. Not long ago, she'd been driving him around, wearing her proper work clothes, and now she was naked in bed and begging for him.

He reached into her bedside table and pulled out the box of Magnums that he'd tossed in her basket the day they met. After rolling on a condom, he slicked himself with lube, then placed the tip of his cock at her entrance.

"Just tell me if I need to stop," he said.

She nodded, but this time, with lots of preparation, he was able to push inside without much difficulty.

"Good girl," he murmured.

God, she felt amazing, so tight around him. He started moving slowly, using his whole body to coax little sighs from her lips, to make her feel as good as he could. He kissed her neck, her mouth, her earlobe. She was wearing pearl studs to match her work outfit, and he found that hot, too.

She arched up, wrapped her legs around his thighs, and took him even deeper.

"Amber, I'm not going to..."

He touched her clit, and they both shuddered together as he rammed into her with a few quick strokes.

He collapsed on his back next to her, head spinning.

"That was incredible," she said, curling up against him.

He put his arm around her and held her close.

Yeah, it had been a pretty incredible night.

# Chapter 6

When Sebastian arrived at his parents' house on Saturday morning, there was already a box of food by the door. No doubt this was for him to take home.

Half the fridge was likely also full of food for him, even though he'd seen them just two days ago. He'd barely had to do any grocery shopping in the last month—except for the time he'd run into Amber.

"Sebastian," Dad said, coming up the stairs from the basement. He was carrying a giant package of toilet paper. "This is for you, too." He placed the toilet paper beside the box. "There was a sale."

Mom hurried to the door. "Don't take off your boots yet!"

Sebastian, unfortunately, had already removed a boot.

"Aiyah." She clucked her tongue. "Okay, put it back on. You need to buy some lightbulbs." She gestured to the light fixture in the front hall. "It is burnt out, and your father bought the wrong ones."

There was a small hardware store on Main Street. Sebastian headed there right away. When he walked out of the store, purchase in hand, his phone buzzed and he reached for it.

The text was from Amber. *Sonata.*

His blood pumped quickly as he pictured her wearing that sexy little vest and pearl earrings...and nothing else. He'd never been turned on by the word "sonata" before.

But.

He was in Ashton Corners visiting his parents. He could not do this right now.

He was about to type out a quick reply when someone said, "Sebastian?"

Sebastian glanced up. There was a middle-aged man coming toward him, and he was the last person on earth Sebastian wanted to see.

"Hello," Stuart said.

*I'm fucking your daughter.*

Of course, Sebastian didn't actually say that—thankfully, he had better control of his mouth—but stood there speechless.

Sebastian had called his man "Uncle Stuart" when he was younger, but the "uncle" part had been dropped over the years.

Suddenly, the fact that he was sleeping with Amber seemed incredibly wrong, even if they were consenting adults who had a good time together.

*Your daughter wants to sext me right now.*

"Hi," Sebastian managed instead. "Good to see you."

Stuart chuckled. "You certainly don't sound happy to see me."

Oh, no.

"Uh, just running some errands for my parents, trying to get back in time for lunch!" Sebastian was rattled and his voice sounded weird to his ears.

He talked to Stuart for a minute before hurrying down Main Street.

When he returned to his parents' house, he changed the lightbulb in the hall light fixture. Both his mom and dad found it necessary to supervise, much to his annoyance.

Then he sent Amber a text. *Sorry, I can't. Maybe tonight.*

He was sitting at the kitchen table while his mother finished cooking lunch when she said, "Who is this friend?"

"What are you talking about?" Sebastian asked, tensing. She hadn't seen him texting Amber, had she?

"You know. The friend you were having bubble tea with when I called on Wednesday."

Ah. Sebastian would have to make something up, and making shit up on the spot was not one of his strengths. But his mother wanted details, so he'd give her details.

"His name is Shane," Sebastian said. "A friend from med school. He, uh, lives in Toronto—that's where he's from—but he was in Waterloo for the day and wanted to meet up."

"What is he doing now?" Mom asked. "Residency? Or is he finished?"

"He's doing his residency in internal medicine."

"Is he married?"

What was with this inquisition?

"Yes," Sebastian decided.

"Did you go to his wedding?"

"No."

"Why not? If you are good enough friends to meet for bubble tea a few years after you have finished med school, why weren't you good enough friends to go to his wedding?

"He got married before med school. Before I met him."

"He must have been very young," Mom said.

"Twenty-three."

"Too young. But you are thirty and have no girlfriend!"

An image of Amber in her vest popped into Sebastian's head again, but he pushed it aside. She wasn't his girlfriend.

"I just got out of a relationship," he said.

"You wasted so many years on Lucinda."

"Wasted" was a bit strong. Though at least they were talking about something real now, rather than Sebastian's imaginary friend named Shane.

This was not what he'd expected adulthood to be like.

"Now you should be in high demand," his mother said. "You are a doctor. You are handsome. Maybe I should start looking for someone for you."

Sebastian sighed. He didn't need his mother involved in his dating life.

Wasn't running into Stuart right after Amber had tried to sext him bad enough?

"Please don't do that, Mom," he said.

"Stuart and Rosemary set their children up with dates for Thanksgiving," Dad said. "Diana went as Zach's date."

"I'm guessing that didn't turn out well or I'd have heard about it before."

Mom lifted the lid on the rice cooker. "Zach did not tell you about this?"

Sebastian felt a stab of guilt at the mention of his friend.

Yes, he really did need to call Zach sometime. He had no social life at present, aside from visiting his parents and having bubble tea with his imaginary friend Shane.

And seeing Amber, of course.

·♥·♥·♥·♥·♥·

"I want one of those," Ah Ma pointed at a cocktail on the waiter's tray.

"I think it's a piña colada," Amber said.

"What is in that? Is there alcohol?"

"Yes. Rum, plus pineapple juice and coconut cream, I believe."

"It looks so cute, with the little umbrella and pineapple slice. Today I am going to be wild and fun like my granddaughter."

Amber's father was working today, and she was having a "girls' day" in London with her mother and grandmother. Ah Ma had seen this on a TV show and decided it needed to happen.

Before driving to London, Amber had attempted to sext Sebastian, thinking that might relieve some of her stress, but unfortunately, he'd been busy.

And now, here she was.

They were at a new restaurant in downtown London, Ontario, and afterward they'd go shopping at Masonville.

"You should have one with me," Ah Ma said to Amber.

"Okay. But just one. I'm driving."

"You, too," Ah Ma said to her daughter-in-law.

Mom shook her head. "No alcohol for me right now."

"Wah, is this the price?" Ah Ma stabbed her finger at the drinks menu. "So expensive."

"It's fine," Mom said. "It's our special day out. And you are only having one drink, because one drink for you is the equivalent of four drinks for someone else."

Ah Ma shook the lunch menu. "I don't understand this. It is supposed to be in English, but I am not so sure? What is chimichurri? What is tartare? This is too complicated. And why are there chocolates in the mac and cheese?"

Amber looked at the description of the mac and cheese and immediately understood her grandmother's confusion. "They aren't talking about chocolate truffles. Truffles are a fancy fungus."

"*Fancy* fungus! In mac and cheese? What do you mean?" Ah Ma shook her head. "White-person restaurants are weird. I am ordering just for me, right? Not for sharing?"

For decades, Ah Ma and Ah Yeh had run Wong's Wok, a Chinese-Canadian restaurant in Mosquito Bay. They'd been so busy working at the restaurant that they hadn't gotten a chance to eat out very often. Besides, there wasn't much selection in Mosquito Bay. When they were in London, Ah Ma usually wanted to go to a Chinese restaurant, but occasionally she could be persuaded to try other things.

However, she ended up complaining most of the time.

Mom sighed. "Maybe this was a mistake. I should have picked something else, but I wanted to give this place a try."

The server came around to take their drink orders, and it was another ten minutes before they decided on their food. Amber ordered the truffle mac and cheese, which came with a spinach salad. Her mother ordered the calamari. Ah Ma chose the lamb burger with sweet potato fries.

Their drinks arrived soon after, and Ah Ma looked at hers with delight.

"Ah, it is so big! And there is the umbrella." Ah Ma took a sip. "It is a little sweet, but still tasty. Amber, take a picture of me enjoying my tropical vacation!"

Dutifully, Amber snapped a picture with her phone.

When the food arrived, Ah Ma didn't even complain about the portion size, which was a definite sign that she had drunk a lot.

Amber had a bite of her salad, then tried the mac and cheese. It was rich and creamy, and she closed her eyes and sighed in bliss.

"It looks like it is delicious," Ah Ma said. "Let me try." She reached over with her fork to grab a bite of Amber's mac and cheese. "Amazing! This is nothing like what comes from the box. I guess fancy fungus is good after all. Rosemary, I am trying some of yours, too." She helped herself to a piece of calamari. "Not as good as the truffle mac and cheese, but still delicious. Can I have some of your drink, too, Amber?"

"You have exactly the same drink as me," Amber pointed out.

"But yours has a blue umbrella! Mine is pink."

"The color of the umbrella doesn't change the taste of the drink."

"Let me test. It will be like a science experiment." Ah Ma grabbed Amber's drink and had a sip. "I think yours is not as sweet as mine."

Mom laughed. "I think you should eat your own food and drink. But I'm glad you like it." She turned to Amber. "How's work going?"

"Pretty good."

"How are Gloria and Roxanne?"

"They're good."

"You know, you can add a little variety to your answers."

"Sorry," Amber said, "I was distracted…"

Her grandmother was triumphantly holding three fries up above her head.

"I am a sweet potato queen!" Ah Ma burped. She had another sweet potato fry, then picked up her burger. She took a big bite of it, and some of the condiments came out the other side. "Such a good burger."

The people at the next table were staring at them.

"So," Mom said to Amber, "Greg, Nick, and Zach all have girlfriends. Are you going to bring a date to Chinese New Year, too?"

"No date," Amber said, "and don't you *dare* set me up with anyone."

"Oh, I wouldn't dare."

"Except you did. At Thanksgiving. With one of my exes."

Mom managed an infuriating smile. "Okay, we did. But I promise, I will not set you up with anyone for Chinese New Year. Maybe we could buy you some nice going-out clothes today, though. Something to really get a guy's attention."

"It's not hard to get a guy's attention. The difficulty is getting a decent man's attention. The dating market is harsh, trust me. I'm off dating at the moment."

"You might meet someone when you least expect it. Like at the grocery store."

Amber choked on her mac and cheese. Her grandma stumbled up from her chair and slapped Amber—with surprising strength—on the back, but unfortunately Ah Ma then tripped on the table leg, and Mom barely got a hold of her before she knocked over one of the piña coladas.

Though Amber was most certainly not dating Sebastian, he was a decent guy, and she'd run into him—for the first time in years—in the grocery store. They'd discussed condoms, not apple varieties or cuts of beef, which was likely what Mom had in mind.

At the horrifying thought of Mom learning the Magnum condom story, Amber took a gulp of her piña colada and almost choked again.

"Went down the wrong pipe," she said. "I'm fine."

"Is there something you're not telling me, Amber?" Mom asked. "Did you, in fact, meet someone at the grocery store?"

"Amber has a mystery man," Ah Ma said gleefully. "Who is he? I will find out."

"No mystery man," Amber said.

But apparently she wasn't convincing enough.

"Does he have big muscles?" Ah Ma flexed her arm before biting into the pineapple garnish on her drink.

"What's his name?" Mom asked. "What does he do for a living?"

"I want to be young again!" Ah Ma said. "Having lots of love affairs. Amber, you should enjoy yourself now. Are you using Tinder? How do these things work? We will get you sexy clothes at the mall today for your mystery man. You will be a hot piece of ass."

"Don't tell my daughter she's a hot piece of ass," Mom said, then started laughing. "You're definitely drunk."

Oh, God. Why was Amber's family even more embarrassing now than when she was a teenager?

Why were they doing this in public?

"We will get you a sexy skirt," Ah Ma said. "Or skort."

Amber just shook her head and looked at her plate. She was losing her appetite.

Her mother and drunk grandmother talked about Amber's love life while they finished their food. The waiter came over and asked if they wanted anything for dessert.

"I will have that," Ah Ma pointed at the table next to them. A woman was drinking a fancy coffee beverage, topped with whipped cream and a cherry.

"I think it has booze," Mom said, "and the last thing you need is more booze."

"We could make booze-free coffee garnished with whipped cream," the waiter said.

"Excellent." Mom smiled at him. "We'll each have one."

"Don't forget the cherries!" Ah Ma said. She grabbed the little umbrellas off the empty cocktail glasses and stuffed them in her purse before the waiter cleared the table.

"Why are you taking the garnish?" Amber asked.

"They are cute! Maybe I will put one in my water glass tonight."

"You know you can buy packages of those. I bet Ah Yeh can find them on Amazon."

"Wah, waste of money when there are two right here. Plus, I want to remember this wonderful girls' day out. These will be a memento. For when I called you a hot piece of ass!"

"I think the coffee will sober her up," Mom whispered to Amber.

"Maybe," Amber said. "But you are perfectly sober and still threatening to get me clothes to help me pick up guys."

The coffee sobered up Ah Ma a little, but she seemed particularly sensitive to the caffeine and started talking a mile a minute. She also had to go to the washroom every ten minutes and kept trying to dance, for mysterious reasons.

Thus, the group shopping trip did not go as planned. It ended after thirty minutes, which was for the best, as Mom's and Ah Ma's taste in clothes had almost no overlap with her Amber's. Also, Ah Ma had insisted they go into a lingerie shop, and Amber had needed to explain how thongs worked.

Not how she'd expected to spend the afternoon.

Once her mother and grandmother were on their way back to Mosquito Bay, Amber did a little shopping on her own. She ended up buying a vest rather similar to the one she'd been wearing when she had bubble tea with Sebastian. Just because it was on sale.

Oh, and Sebastian would like it. Whenever she thought about wearing it for him, it brought a stupid grin to her face. Maybe she could wear it with nothing underneath.

Lingerie was a relationship thing to Amber, but a vest was *not* lingerie.

After leaving the mall, she figured she might as well make another stop while she was in London. She went to Glazed, a gourmet donut shop, and enjoyed a red velvet donut—her favorite—as she recovered from seeing her family.

As she licked the cream cheese frosting off her fingers, she thought of Sebastian again. Imagined licking frosting off his long pianist's fingers. Wondered if he'd be free to sext later.

That evening, after a few drinks at The Tempest with her friends, Amber went home, changed into her pajamas, and took her phone to bed with her.

*Hey*, she texted Sebastian.

She waited. And waited.

Amber organized the top drawer of her night table—the one with the sex toys and condoms—and still her phone didn't buzz.

She picked up her phone to check that she hadn't set it to silent.

No, she hadn't.

She tried not to feel disappointed.

She was about to get up to brush her teeth when her phone finally vibrated.

*Sorry about earlier,* he texted. *I was in Ashton Corners, and a few seconds after I got your text, I ran into your dad.*

Oh, dear. That sounded as painfully uncomfortable as her day.

*I was out with my mom and grandmother. Mom suggested I might meet someone when I least expect it. Like at the grocery store. Ah Ma got drunk on a single piña colada and said she wanted me to look like a hot piece of ass.*

*You want me to help you forget about it all?* he asked.

*Please.*

*I have a question for you first. Want to come over tomorrow night? I'll cook dinner.*

*Sounds like a date,* she replied.

*It's not. You took me out for bubble tea and fried chicken, so I can make a meal for you, right? How's 7?*

*Works for me.* Amber's hand drifted over her body, from her breasts to her thighs. *Sonata.* She waited for his reply, her heart thumping too fast.

*Where are you?* he asked.

*In bed. Wearing pajamas.*

*I want you to lick your finger...*

Oh, hell, yes. She'd been waiting for this all day.

She did as he asked and got comfortable under the covers, ready for more.

# Chapter 7

Sebastian was nervous.

He shouldn't be nervous. This wasn't a date.

Which had made it difficult to figure out what to cook. Pasta seemed romantic, as did mussels. Fried rice wasn't romantic, but it didn't seem fancy enough.

What was it that made pasta more romantic than fried rice? Hmm.

He had a nice chicken dish that he'd made for dates in the past, but he didn't like the idea of making something he'd cooked for a date before, even if this was, decisively, *not* a date. Also, it was a little fussy. This meal should be simple, something that didn't scream, *I spent all day in the kitchen for you!* But also not something that said, *I just tossed any old thing into the frying pan.*

In the end, he'd decided on a lentil-sausage soup. But what if she didn't like soup?

Once, he would have thought that impossible, but his ex hadn't liked soup of any kind, and it had driven him mad. They hadn't been able to go out for ramen or pho.

Perhaps he should have asked Amber what she preferred.

He remembered from their childhood that she hated broccoli, but that could have changed. Though to be safe, he hadn't made anything with broccoli.

The doorbell rang, and he padded down the hallway to answer it.

Amber looked around after taking off her boots. Sebastian lived in a small house that was a short drive from her apartment. It was clear he hadn't lived here long. Not because there were piles of boxes, but because it was a bit sparse. Like it needed some homey touches. Perhaps she could make him a cross-stitch that said, *Welcome to my den of pleasure.*

"What's so funny?" Sebastian asked.

"Oh, nothing," she said. "It smells good."

He led her to the dining room table, where there were two empty bowls, spoons, butter, and a small pile of crusty rolls. He placed a large pot on a trivet.

"I made lentil-sausage soup with kale," he said, ladling them each a bowl.

They sat in silence as they waited for the soup to cool, Sebastian constantly dipping his spoon into the soup and letting it drip off, Amber tearing her dinner roll and buttering it.

This was weird. Why was this weird? Was it because just last night, they'd sent each other naughty text messages?

Nah, she didn't think that was it.

She tried some soup.

"It's delicious," she said.

"Thank you." His voice was unsteady.

They'd already slept together and sexted, but she hadn't been to his place before, and they were having a home-cooked meal for the first time. Perhaps he was nervous.

"You wanted to feed me something with sausages, didn't you?" she said. "Except the sausages in the soup are cut up, so I can't see whether they were long and extra-thick. Were they *magnum* sausages?"

God, she sounded like she was drunk on a piña colada.

Sebastian lifted a spoonful of soup to his mouth, then snorted and put down the spoon. He started laughing as she'd never heard him laugh before. He chuckled a lot, sure, but this was a full-on belly-aching laugh, and she couldn't help the warmth that spread through her body. Though perhaps he was laughing like this mainly because of his nervousness, which was kind of cute, actually...

*Friends*, she reminded herself. *Friends make friends laugh.*

He squeezed her hand, then went back to eating his soup.

She could get used to this. A nice, casual dinner at the end of a workday with Sebastian.

*Friends!* she screamed inside her head. *This is friendship, not romance.*

"Amber?" Sebastian said, his eyebrows drawing together. "Is everything okay?"

"Oh, yes, everything is great, thank you!" Her voice sounded a little too chipper, but he didn't comment on it.

After dinner, Sebastian brought out some candy cane ice cream, the kind she'd had in her basket at the grocery store two weeks ago.

Two weeks? Weirdly, it seemed both longer and shorter at the same time.

Everything was going great so far. They'd been having sex about twice a week—and regular sex was exactly what she needed.

She had a generous serving of ice cream, then stood up and slid onto his lap.

"You're wearing too much clothing," she declared.

"Am I?"

"Mm-hmm. I think it's time I did something about it. To thank you for the great meal."

And that was exactly what she did.

·♥·♥·♥·♥·♥·

It was nine o'clock, and Sebastian had stuff he should probably be doing—dishes, for example—but instead he was lying in bed with Amber, her head resting on his shoulder.

His bedroom seemed boring compared to hers. There were no crochet peacocks on the bedside table, no cross-stitched rules above the bed.

"What's rule number two?" he asked suddenly. "Rule number one is no dating...what's rule number two?"

"Yet to be determined," she said. "I'm keeping my options open."

He pulled her closer. It was a touch drafty in his bedroom, and they were snuggled up under a mound of blankets...and there was nowhere else he'd rather be.

"You said you're taking a break from dating because you tend to date terrible men."

"Yes." She sighed. "I really do. Any type of bad boyfriend you can think of, I've had."

"Cheaters?"

"That goes without saying. One guy claimed he was single but turned out to have a wife and two small children. I also dated a man who thought women shouldn't be able to vote."

"He didn't think women should *vote*?"

"He only said that once. When he was drunk. Went on a rant about how women were too liberal and didn't know what was good for them. I bet that was how he truly felt; he just knew better than to spout those views when he was sober. Then there were a couple of white guys who had creepy Asian fetishes. One thought I should be more in touch with my culture and mocked me for some of the non-traditional food I made. The other thought I should be submissive. When I dumped him, he blamed my lack of meek and polite personality on me being..." She shook her head. "I won't repeat what he said. Slurs against people who are biracial."

Sebastian's hand tightened on Amber's arm, but then he realized he might be hurting her. He let go and soothed her skin with his fingers. "I can't believe you dated those guys."

"I'm incredibly dumb."

"That's not what I meant."

"You don't have to lie. I was young, I liked men, I wasn't too picky. I enjoyed the attention."

"I'm sure they didn't act like total jerks when you first met them."

"No, but I should have known better. Especially when I..." She shut her eyes for a moment. "You can't tell Zach or anyone else in my family, okay?"

"Okay."

"I dated a few men who were quite a bit older than me. Like, when I was nineteen, I dated a guy who was thirty-five. Older than you are now. He made me feel grown-up. I wanted people to see me as something other than the baby of the family, wanted them to take me seriously. It felt like he did. Then he dumped me for someone who was only seventeen." She shifted against Sebastian. "I also dated a professor."

"While he was teaching you?"

"No, afterward. Well, we kissed once when I was taking his class, but it didn't really start until the next semester. I know, I was stupid."

"It's not you. It's him. He was your professor."

"Yeah, it was fucked up. But it felt like I had a dirty little secret, and I loved it...for a few weeks. He was kind of an ass, to be honest, and he had another girlfriend. Anyway, that's why I've taken a break from dating for nearly a year now."

"Have you've enjoyed it?"

"It's been good. More time to spend with friends, crochet, and watch Netflix. I feel like I have a better handle on who I am. Only problem was that I missed sex, but I have that now." She tapped his naked ass.

"Do you plan to date again?"

"Oh, sure. I haven't sworn off dating for the rest of my life. Just figured I could use a long break. Hopefully, when I start dating again, I'll be better at seeing past bullshit."

It seemed like she was pretty good at seeing past bullshit now.

She sounded matter-of-fact and cautiously optimistic that one day, it would work out. He couldn't help being impressed she'd gone through all that and become the person he'd gotten to know over the past two weeks. Fun, joyful, thoughtful, and down-to-earth. He knew she could survive more shit, but he wanted to prevent her from going through it again.

He was about to—jokingly, of course—suggest he vet her potential boyfriends, but he couldn't get the words out. The idea of her being with someone else was difficult to think about.

"None of them were as big as you," she said, "in case you were wondering."

"I wasn't. That would be odd."

"I don't know, men are weird about dick size. Why did I end up dating multiple men who were convinced they needed Magnums but didn't?" She stretched out next to him. "What about you? Have you dated a lot of women?"

"Just a few."

"My dating history must seem rather excessive to you."

"No, I'm not judging."

*It made you who you are today, and I think you're amazing.*

This was the truth, but he wasn't sure why he was quite so sappy about it.

He didn't say anything else for a few minutes, just enjoyed having her in his bed. It was getting late, though, and they both had to work tomorrow.

"You want to stay the night?" he asked, surprising himself.

"No, I should probably be going."

He tried not to be disappointed.

# Chapter 8

Wednesday after dinner, Amber was watching a baking show and working on her latest crochet project when the TV and lights suddenly went out.

No big deal. The power would probably just be off for a few minutes.

She took out her phone and looked at a houseplant forum. She'd joined it on a whim last summer when her fern was dying.

She had yet to make a single post.

She was, quite frankly, terrified to do so. Who would have thought that houseplant enthusiasts would be so vicious? But they were. Someone had posted a picture of their succulent the other day, and there had been a heated debate over what type of succulent it was. Last week, a woman had managed to kill a cactus, and oh my God, she'd gotten destroyed.

Amber, for whatever reason, enjoyed the low-stakes and high-drama debates.

She'd also learned quite a bit about ferns and had managed to figure out what was wrong with hers, but she would never, ever post her own question.

After looking through the houseplant forum, she went to Instagram. She followed a bunch of bakers who posted pictures of their amazing cakes, and there was a spectacular geode cake today.

Finally, Amber got tired of social media, and her phone battery was running low.

And the power still hadn't come back on.

She looked at the Twitter feed for the hydro company, which confirmed that yes, there was a localized outage, and they expected it to last until midnight, maybe later.

Midnight! It was only eight thirty now. What would Amber do for the next three hours? And what if the power wasn't back on by tomorrow morning?

Maybe she could stay with Gloria.

She texted her friend but didn't get a response, and actually, that was a bit of a relief.

Because now she could ask Sebastian.

She figured Sebastian would be home on a Wednesday night, and he'd let her stay—after all, he'd asked her to stay on Sunday.

She'd said no. Although she didn't have strict rules about not staying overnight with a guy other than a boyfriend, it had seemed a little relationship-y for her comfort.

But now, her power was out. It was only sensible.

She texted Sebastian, and she got a reply a couple minutes later.

*Sure, come on over.*

Amber could barely contain her grin.

She needed to make sure they focused on sex, with a side of friendship. Nothing romantic about tonight at all. No snuggling up while they watched a movie.

She had better ideas.

Amber set down her overnight bag and slipped off her winter boots.

"Hey," Sebastian said, his hands slung in the pouch of his hoodie. "Sorry about your power."

"Are you?" she asked, sliding her hands under his sweatshirt and T-shirt.

She couldn't think straight now that she was touching him, especially not after what she'd done before leaving her apartment. It had been hard to get dressed in the dark, and it had taken a while to find what she needed.

She kissed him hard on the lips, and he growled.

"I have something to show you," she said coyly. "Let's go upstairs."

"Lead the way." His rough voice vibrated inside her.

Once they were in the bedroom, she pushed him down on the bed so that he was lying on his back, his head on the pillows.

Then she stood at the foot of the bed and tossed her sweatshirt on the floor.

He breathed in sharply.

She wasn't wearing anything particularly revealing. Just a skirt, a button-down white shirt with one—okay, maybe two—more buttons undone that was strictly proper. Plus the vest she'd bought the other day. Some minor adjustments and she could wear this to the office.

"You like it?" she asked.

"You look hot." He leaned forward and reached for her.

"Uh-uh. You only get to touch when I tell you to."

The corner of his mouth quirked up. "Okay."

She wasn't entirely sure what she was doing, but she'd wanted to wear something he'd like, and she wanted to be in charge for a little. The other day, when he'd cooked her dinner and they'd talked for a long time in bed, she'd felt like she was losing some control of the situation.

But not now.

They were going to *fuck*.

His gaze raked over her, and he licked his lips.

She got a thrill out of turning him on, more than what she'd experienced with other men.

Discarding that thought, she crawled across the bed toward him, her hands and legs staying on either side of his body.

And...*oh*.

"You okay?" he asked.

"Yeah, I'm fine." She wouldn't tell him why she'd winced, not yet.

He was looking down her shirt—he must have a good view of her cleavage in this position—and she watched his Adam's apple bob as he swallowed. He kept his hands fisted in the blanket when she touched his cheek and kissed him, her tongue stroking against his.

Next, she got to work on his jeans. She unbuckled his belt, unzipped the zipper, and slid her hand over the hot length of him.

He hissed and tore his mouth away from hers.

*Oh, just you wait.* She'd hardly gotten started.

She moved to his side and took his erection—as much of it as she could—in her mouth.

He gripped her hair and moved her up and down on his cock. When she squirmed, the toy shifted inside her, and she groaned.

Fuck.

She couldn't wait any longer. She rolled off him, removed her skirt and panties...and watched his eyes widen. To give him the full effect, she stood up beside the bed and clenched her inner muscles.

She was wearing a dress shirt and vest, but her tits were almost hanging out, and the end of a dildo stuck out of her.

He looked at her with *very* appreciative shock.

Sebastian was the good son, who'd gone to medical school and hadn't given up on piano lessons but instead got his ARCT.

And here he was, mouth hanging open, pants undone, watching with rapt attention as Amber pumped a toy in and out of her body.

She took a moment to savor the situation.

She felt like she was the bad girl corrupting him, even though that wasn't true. He hadn't had as many sexual partners as she had, but he'd been in relationships and was clearly experienced in making a woman feel good.

And though Amber's life was actually quite respectable now—decent apartment, decent job—in this position, she felt anything but respectable, and it was a great feeling. Empowering.

Yes, with him, she had power. He wasn't some asshole with weird and possibly racist preconceived notions of who she should be. They'd known each other for a long time, but—perhaps because they hadn't seen each other in nine years—she could be who she wanted with him and know he'd see her that way. The way she wanted to be seen.

He yanked off his shirt and crawled toward the edge of the bed. She breathed in swiftly, her attention focused on the swell of his biceps, his erection bobbing between his legs.

And the toy inside her, of course.

He came to sit in front of her on the bed, his feet planted on the ground.

"You," he whispered, "are incredible. That toy looks so fucking pretty in your pussy."

Her skin sparked at his words. She loved when he talked to her like this. When he was filthy, rather than the proper man the world saw.

He grasped the end of the dildo. "May I?"

Filthy, but polite.

"Please."

Slowly, he slid it in and out of her. His gaze was riveted on hers, as though he was memorizing every quick gasp, every flutter of her eyelids.

"God, you're so sexy." His other hand moved over her ass, kneading and squeezing. "Naughty girl." He gave her a light slap.

Then he let go of the toy and unbuttoned her vest, followed by her shirt. These, and her bra, were tossed on the carpet before he returned to sliding the toy inside her.

"Sebastian," she moaned. "I can't...I'm not going to..." Her legs started to quiver.

"Come to bed," he murmured, scooping her ass toward him. She fell on top of him, laughing. "On your elbows and knees."

It wasn't a command. Well, not what *she* thought of as a command. His words were quiet, and not firm—but not weak, either. It wasn't a question—and yet it was. *If it will please you, this is what I want you to do.*

She wasn't in control anymore, and yet she was.

She did exactly as he said, her face toward the foot of the bed, her ass toward the pillows. She sensed him adjusting himself behind her.

"Good girl," he said.

She was acutely aware of every inch of her bare skin; it felt overly sensitized.

"Touch me," she whispered.

Sebastian would touch her soon, but for now, he'd simply enjoy the delectable image in front of him.

Thank God for power outages.

Amber hadn't simply thrown a few things in a bag and come over to his well-lit home. No, she'd put on a special outfit just for him.

The toy he'd used on her the very first time. Sexy work clothes, similar to the one she'd worn for bubble tea, which he'd professed to like very much.

For him.

And for her, of course. He knew she wouldn't be doing this if she didn't enjoy it.

There were so many things he wished to do to her.

"You're face-down on my bed with your ass in the air," he observed. "Is that because you need a spanking?"

He could tell from the hitch in her breath that she liked the idea, but he waited for her to speak.

"Yes," she said.

He wouldn't spank her hard, but God, he was desperate to see his hand hit her ass.

First, he palmed her ass gently, then raised his hand up.

He smacked her.

She trembled.

"Okay?" he asked.

Her head was pressed against the bed, but she nodded.

So he spanked her again. Twice. Three times. Four times.

"Sebastian," she said, begging, but she didn't say for what.

He pulled the dildo out of her and replaced it with two fingers, hissing when he discovered that she was dripping wet. The fact that she was so turned on...it turned him on even further.

"Good girl," he murmured. "So good."

He shed the rest of his clothes and sat behind her. Pressed his mouth to her entrance, fucked her with his tongue, then swirled his tongue over her clit. Again and again....

"Sebastian!" she cried, her hands gripping the blankets.

Over the past couple weeks, he'd learned that Amber could come a few times in close proximity—usually with clitoral stimulation.

"Another?" he said.

"Yes."

He jacked himself off with one hand while the other thrust the dildo into her body. He loved how it looked coming out of her channel. When he pressed his finger to her swollen nub, she jumped and came immediately, sobbing against the blanket, her knees sliding back until she was lying on her stomach, unable to support herself.

He lay on top of her, pressing kisses over her neck and face. "Do you want more, love? Or are you finished?"

"Let me get you off first. You wanted to see my mouth on your cock, didn't you?"

He could only nod.

She took a few deep breaths, recovering, before pushing him onto his back and wrapping her lips around his erection.

He ran his hand through her hair and murmured, "You're incredible... You're so good at taking my cock... God, yes."

He didn't last long. Soon, his entire body was pulsing with his orgasm, and a shout ripped from his mouth, catching him off guard.

"*Amber.*"

When he found his bearings again, he realized the dildo was still inside her. Her pussy had been full when she'd sucked him off.

Oh, fuck. He jammed it into her again and again as he devoured her mouth and squeezed her breasts and tried to give her all the pleasure in the world.

And when she screamed for him, he was filled with bliss.

Amber felt like she was drunk, though she hadn't had a drop of alcohol tonight.

But she was giddy and light-headed, and she couldn't stop smiling and laughing. She'd had plenty of satisfying sex before, but it had never made her feel quite like *this*.

She nestled against Sebastian. He was grinning too, looking mighty pleased with himself for what he'd done to her. She wanted to kiss him, and so she did, leisurely stroking her tongue into his mouth.

Afterward, she couldn't help giggling again.

Her body, though, was utterly boneless with satisfaction. She'd already gotten up to go to the washroom, and she didn't plan on standing up again for a long time.

"You wore me out," she said.

And she drifted off in his arms.

Sebastian was a bit of a morning person, though he would have happily stayed in bed for longer today, tangled up with Amber.

However, they both had to work.

He'd showered quickly, and now she was showering while he made her breakfast.

Coffee was already brewing. Normally he'd have cold cereal during the week, but he figured he had enough time to make French toast. Thankfully, he had the ingredients for this unexpected romantic mid-week breakfast.

Romantic?

For Sunday's dinner, he'd been very careful to make sure it wasn't romantic, but now he was making French toast with maple syrup and strawberries and baked banana, and he was *whistling*.

He wiped his hands on a towel and glanced at the perfect slices of strawberries he'd cut, determined to make sure their plates looked just right. He couldn't help wishing that it wasn't dark out, and that he had a little glass vase of flowers. Daisies, maybe.

Sebastian wasn't used to lying to himself, but he realized he'd been doing a little of that lately.

But no longer.

He was falling in love with Amber Wong.

He certainly hadn't expected this to happen, just after he'd moved to Stratford, only a few months after his break-up with Lucinda.

Yet there it was.

Funny that you fucked a woman with a dildo and it made you realize you were falling in love with her.

Though, frankly, it had started when she drove him to Waterloo to have bubble tea, if not before.

He brought the coffee and mugs to the table on a tray, and he was about to plate the French toast when Amber came into the kitchen. She was wearing black pants, a white shirt—and God, the vest she'd worn yesterday. Her hair was wet, and she had a towel over her shoulders.

"You don't have a hair dryer," she said.

No, he kept his hair quite short and didn't need one.

He made a mental note to buy a hair dryer this weekend.

"I might have thought of it if I'd had more time to pack, but there was the blackout, and..." She shrugged. "The power's back on, supposedly."

"That's good." Though he would have been happy to have her back here tonight.

"It smells great. What did you make?"

He held out a plate with two pieces of French toast and two long slices of baked banana. She hadn't been impressed with his banana milk tea, but she'd said she liked cooked bananas, and he didn't have much other fruit in the house. There were sliced strawberries scattered over the French toast, and a few more in the corner of the plate.

"Sebastian, you garnished it!" She took the plate and kissed his cheek.

He could get used to this. Waking up with Amber, having breakfast with her, seeing her dressed up before she went to work...

Oh, yes. He wanted a whole lot more than this arrangement offered.

Perhaps the fact that she was happy about breakfast was a sign that she might be interested in something more, too.

After all, it wasn't like Amber was completely against dating. She'd just wanted to take a break after all her shitty experiences with men.

Which she'd told him about.

Perhaps that was also a sign that she wanted to be closer to him.

Or it was a sign that they were friends, and her delight over breakfast was just a sign that she was hungry.

Hmm.

He knew he was better than the boyfriends she'd told him about the other day. This had nothing to do with size, of course. He wasn't a white boy with a creepy fetish; he believed in equal rights; he wasn't sixteen years older and in a position of power over her.

Okay, the bar was low, but he knew he'd treat her right.

He sat down with his plate of food and put the pitcher of maple syrup on the table. Yes, he'd actually poured the maple syrup into a small pitcher rather than putting the bottle on the table. He sure was being fancy.

"This banana is good," Amber said. "It's so sweet and melts in your mouth. You used butter didn't you?"

Watching her eat his food was making him a little hard, but he didn't think they had time to do it before work.

"Do you enjoy cooking?" he asked instead, wanting to know more about her.

"I don't mind it on occasion, but I don't like having to think about meals every day. It's one of the things I hate about being an adult—you always have to figure out what to eat for breakfast, lunch, and dinner. I wish someone would do it all for me for a few weeks."

He held himself back from volunteering.

"Actually..." She had a bite of French toast before continuing. "You know what I want to get into? Cakes. I love watching baking shows. I want to make and decorate fancy cakes. There's a class I could take in Waterloo, but..." She shrugged.

"Why not? Is it too expensive?"

"It's more that it seems like a silly hobby, and it's not like I'd ever do it for a living."

"You don't think you'd be good enough?"

"No, I just don't have an interest in doing it professionally. I prefer my current job to working in a kitchen."

"There's nothing wrong with doing things for fun. If you don't want to take the class alone, I could do it with you."

The words had just popped out of his mouth.

And that's how he knew he was really falling in love. Sebastian had no interest in cakes and cake decorating. He appreciated the taste of a good cake, but he'd always thought elaborate wedding cakes and such were silly.

But it sounded fun…if it was with her.

When should he broach the issue of them being a real couple?

Amber had a sip of coffee, then spontaneously burst into giggles, as she had so many times in his arms last night.

"Imagine if our parents found us eating breakfast together," she said.

"Fortunately, my parents are unlikely to surprise me with a visit at seven in the morning."

"But if we did this on the weekend and were, say, having brunch at ten, it wouldn't be out of the question. My parents usually call before they visit, but occasionally they don't. They'd ask lots of questions and would interfere so much. My family is always jumping to conclusions and getting carried away. If my grandma saw us eating breakfast together, she'd probably be planning the wedding." Amber shuddered.

"My parents, too."

"No, your parents hate me."

What?

"Of course they don't," he said.

"Okay, maybe that was a bit strong, but they're not my biggest fans. I work for a theater festival—that's not respectable enough for them. They were perturbed by my so-called wild antics in high school. I'm positive they don't think I'm good enough for you."

"Our parents are good friends. They'd be thrilled."

She shook her head. "Our families can't find out. They'd get the wrong idea—mine would be happy, yours wouldn't—and I don't want to tell them what's actually going on. Your parents would definitely think I was a bad influence."

It was clear she wouldn't be receptive to the idea of a relationship with him.

If they were in a real relationship, they'd have to tell their families eventually. He agreed that their families would be a little annoying, but it seemed like a small price to pay for being with Amber. And in a way, it was nice that their families were already friends. There would be no uncomfortable meet-the-parents-for-the-first-time dinners—because they already knew each other's parents.

He still didn't believe his parents would be unhappy, as she assumed.

Well. Now was not the time to ask Amber about being a couple. He would say something eventually, but not yet.

# Chapter 9

"LET'S SEE IF I'VE got this right," Gloria said. "There was a blackout on Wednesday night, I wasn't responding, so you went to Sebastian's and stayed overnight?"

"Yep." Amber sipped her beer. "What else was I going to do until bedtime?"

"You could have hung out at Tim Hortons. Or here." Gloria took off her black fedora and gestured to their surroundings. "You could have spent the evening staring at Justin Bieber." She pointed at the poster on the wall.

"Or I could have had sex. It was an easy decision. What's wrong with a booty call?"

"Nothing," Gloria said. "But you could have returned home to sleep, yet you stayed. Just trying to figure out what's going on."

"What happened the next morning?" Roxanne asked.

"He made me coffee and French toast with baked bananas," Amber said morosely, knowing how her friends would take it.

"He likes you. He definitely likes you."

"No," Amber protested. "He's just a sweet guy, that's all."

"You think he makes French toast for every booty call?" Gloria asked.

"I don't think Sebastian has many booty calls, to be honest."

"Yet he made an exception for you."

"We agreed it's just sex."

"Perhaps he thought that at the beginning," Roxanne said. "But French toast? With baked bananas?"

"And a strawberry garnish." Amber wasn't sure why she mentioned that. It was adding fuel to the fire.

"*He garnished your fucking breakfast?*" Gloria spoke as though this was truly shocking information. "None of my boyfriends or girlfriends have done that for me."

Amber's lips twitched at her friend's vehemence. "Well, they should. You deserve a strawberry garnish."

"Ha!" Gloria said. "You didn't protest and say he isn't your boyfriend."

Oops. She hadn't. It didn't mean anything, though.

"I'm drunk. My brain isn't operating at a hundred percent."

"Oh, come on. You're only on your second pint. You're not that cheap of a drunk."

"Personally," Roxanne said, "I think the baked bananas are a bigger deal than the strawberries. Slicing up strawberries takes a minute. Baking bananas requires more effort."

"But less hands-on time," Gloria countered. "No, strawberries are inherently romantic. If a guy serves you strawberries, he knows what he's doing. Bananas might have been meant as a dirty joke. Like, he wants you to bake his banana."

"What does that even mean?" Amber asked.

"Who knows. I just made it up."

"Anyway," Roxanne said, after raising an eyebrow at Gloria, "this guy definitely has a crush on Amber. On that we agree."

"Yep." Gloria took a swig of her beer. "Amber, this guy wants you for more than your hot body and great skills in the sack. I'm positive."

"And you definitely want him, too," Roxanne added.

"Have you not been listening to anything I've said?" Amber curled her hands in frustration. "We're fucking, and we like each other's company. I don't want anything romantic."

"Then why have we been talking about this for twenty minutes?" Gloria demanded.

"Hey, this wasn't my choice of conversation."

"But you keep adding interesting details." Roxanne crossed her arms over her chest. "I think you secretly want him, but you're in denial."

"My thoughts exactly," Gloria said. "The reason you keep bringing up all the things he's done—"

"Is because I'm drunk!" Amber protested.

Thank God she had enough presence of mind not to mention the cake decorating class.

"I don't buy it," Gloria said. "You enjoy being teased about this guy because you liiiiike him."

"Stop it," Amber said, without any force behind her words.

She most certainly did not enjoy all this teasing...did she?

She doubted herself for a moment, then shook her head. Nope, she didn't enjoy it. Time for a new topic of conversation.

"Hey." The voice was lower than either Roxanne's or Gloria's.

Amber turned and saw a man standing beside her, with glasses and a rather cute nerdy look. He ran a hand over his face, as though nervous.

"Hey." She smiled at him.

"I...uh...can I buy you a drink?" He gestured to her nearly-empty pint. "What are you drinking?"

Amber's instincts when it came to men had failed her many, *many* times in the past, but she was older now, and she was convinced she was getting better at this.

And this guy seemed sweet and looked like Chidi from *The Good Place*.

However, she didn't feel even a flicker of interest.

"Sorry," she said kindly. "I have a boyfriend."

"Really, she does," Gloria piped up. "It's not just a line. I mean, the guy's not officially her boyfriend, but she sleeps over at his place—"

"Only because of the blackout," Amber said.

"—and he makes her romantic breakfasts."

"They're not romantic."

"Tell me." Gloria turned to the man. "If you made French toast with baked bananas and strawberries for a woman who spent the night, would that mean you had romantic feelings toward her?"

"Uh, yeah?"

"See, Amber?" Gloria grinned triumphantly. "Told you."

The man returned to his friends on the other side of the bar.

"Do you and Sebastian have any cute nicknames for each other?" Roxanne asked.

"I bet you call him Sebbie, don't you?" Gloria said. "How sweet!"

"I don't think he'd like that," Amber said.

"Nah, I'm sure he'd find it cute if *you* called him Sebbie."

Amber felt her lips curve into a smile, then quickly put a stop to that instinctive facial expression. Her friends would read too much into it.

"Have you done lots of dirty things together?" Gloria asked. "Did you grapefruit him?"

"Um...."

"Didn't you see *Girls Trip*? Is his dick so big that it requires two grapefruits?"

Amber found herself considering the size of an average grapefruit relative to the size of Sebastian's dick...then told her brain to behave. "I'm not dicknifying that with a response."

Gloria slapped her hand against the table. "You said 'dicknifying'!"

"No, I said 'dignifying'."

"Gloria's right," Roxanne said.

"It's the alcohol." Amber nodded at her glass. She was getting sick of all the teasing, and her friends were delusional. "Hey, there's a play I want to see in Toronto next month. Anyone want to come with me?"

"You could bring—" Gloria began.

"No, I'm not bringing *Sebbie*. But you could ask Syd. Things are still going well, right? And you've reached the six-month mark now?"

Amber was pleased things were working out for Gloria. But her and Sebastian? That wasn't the same.

·❤·❤·❤·❤·❤·

When Amber got home on Saturday after her family's Chinese New Year dinner, she brushed her teeth, changed into her pajamas, and snuggled under the covers, phone in hand.

*Hey,* she texted Sebastian. *You'll never guess what happened tonight.*

She stared at her phone for two minutes, willing it to vibrate.

*What?* he replied at last, and she couldn't help smiling.

*You know how my family always plays Pictionary at Chinese New Year? Zach's new girlfriend got "shaft," and she drew an enormous picture of a dick. In front of my entire family.*

*LOL. Were your grandparents scandalized?*

*Yeah, I think they were.*

*How did your team do?* he asked.

*I wasn't on a team. As the only one who wasn't part of a couple, I got to be scorekeeper.*

Which she hadn't minded. It meant Zach didn't bug her about her drawing skills.

She suddenly realized she'd spent her entire drive home looking forward to telling Sebastian about a Pictionary game. It didn't mean she *liked* him, but... Her excitement about telling him was disturbing, nonetheless.

Time to make this sexual.

She opened the top drawer of her night table and sent him another text.

*Speaking of big dicks...*

Wednesday evening, Amber saw Sebastian again.

Thursday evening, she was sitting in front of her TV, watching a baking competition and trying to decide what to crochet next.

Sebastian had liked her little peacock. Maybe she could make something for him. But what would be best? Which animal was his favorite?

Okay, she had to admit that she liked Sebastian a teeny-tiny bit as something other than a friend. She was thinking of doing a crochet project for him, which wasn't the sort of thing she did for Gloria or Roxanne.

But this could never become anything more.

First of all, she was off dating at the moment. Now, it had been nearly a year, and the reason she'd stopped dating was because she was the Queen of Bad Boyfriends—and Sebastian was nothing like her exes. He was a good guy.

He'd made her French toast for breakfast. With baked fruit and a garnish.

He was thoughtful and considerate in the bedroom...in a totally ungentlemanly way. She squeezed her thighs together at the thought of what they'd done together last night. He'd blindfolded her with one of his ties and pleasured her for half an hour, until she was begging for his cock. He'd whispered such naughty things in her ear...

She'd assumed they'd sleep together a couple times and that would be it. Except it had been going on for a few weeks now, and she had no desire to end it. This was exactly the sex she needed.

And, okay, there was that teeny-tiny feeling of romance.

Her friends had a point, much as it pained her to admit it.

Sebastian would not be the bad boyfriend she was afraid of, but was she ready for a relationship? With a Lam?

That was the big problem. She might be interested in dipping her toe back into the world of romance, but with Sebastian, she couldn't simply dip her toe. Their families would make sure of it.

They could avoid telling their families for a little while, but not forever, especially since Sebastian was an honest guy who didn't like keeping secrets.

He'd asked her if he could tell Zach there was something going on between them—because he was seeing Zach this weekend and would feel weird about his friend not knowing—and Amber had said yes, as long as it was vague and Zach swore not to tell anyone else.

She wasn't sure how Zach would take this. He was her older brother, after all, but Sebastian thought it wouldn't be a big deal, and she was trying to believe him.

Their parents absolutely couldn't know, however.

Besides, she only liked Sebastian a teeny-tiny bit, and maybe she should stop seeing him soon, to prevent those feelings from becoming anything more.

No, she wouldn't make him a peacock.

Sebastian drove back to Stratford, whistling along to the music in the car.

After visiting his parents this afternoon, he'd stopped by Zach's house in Mosquito Bay and told his friend that he was seeing Amber. To his relief, Zach had been fine with it. This was what Sebastian had expected, although he hadn't been entirely confident.

With Zach, Sebastian had pretended he didn't know where things were headed with Amber, though that wasn't true. He knew he was falling in love, but he hadn't wanted to say it out loud until he'd spoken to her, and that wouldn't be for a couple more weeks.

Valentine's Day.

Yes, Sebastian had finally settled on a date.

Sure, Valentine's Day might be a little cheesy and predictable, but he liked the idea of it. It seemed fitting, since her basket had been full of discounted Christmas chocolate when they'd met at the grocery store, that this involved another holiday. Plus, Valentine's Day was on a Friday this year. The timing was good.

Until then, he'd be very sweet—except in the bedroom—and prove he was the guy she deserved.

He just hoped she'd be interested, and he hoped he could reassure her that his parents would like her and wouldn't interfere *that* much.

# Chapter 10

"YOU WILL NEVER GUESS what happened!" Ah Ma said.

Amber held the phone closer to her ear as she reclined on her couch. "What?"

"Guess!"

"No, I'm not playing this game."

"Fine, be no fun," Ah Ma said. "Zach's relationship was fake. Jo wasn't his girlfriend."

Amber sighed. "I already knew that." Her mother had called her the other day.

She'd been surprised. Zach and Jo had seemed like a real couple at Chinese New Year. However, she could understand Zach's desire to avoid further matchmaking.

"You already knew?" Ah Ma shouted. "Aiyah. I thought I had big exciting news! But did you hear the rest of the story? They are now together for real. It is like a novel! Maybe you should get a fake relationship and turn it into a real one."

Zach and Jo's story did sound sweet, yes. However, Amber was not interested in doing that herself.

"Guess what I am doing now?" This time, Ah Ma didn't give Amber a chance to respond. "I am having orange juice in a glass with a little umbrella. I use the umbrellas every time I have water or juice."

"You mean the cocktail umbrellas from the time we had piña coladas?

"Yes! That was a great day, wasn't it?"

"To be honest," Amber said, "I'm surprised you remember any of it."

"Silly girl! Of course I remember. I had a piña colada, and it was delicious! Then I went home and had a long nap."

"Do you remember going to the mall?"

"We didn't go to the mall."

"Yes, we went to Masonville. You don't remember because you were drunk. You were trying to get me to wear clothes that would make me look like a hot piece of ass."

"Wah, don't use those naughty words."

"I'm just repeating what you said."

"Hmm," Ah Ma said. "I guess it sounds like something I might say if I was drunk. So, did it work? Do you have a boyfriend now?"

"No boyfriend."

Why did that feel like a lie? It wasn't a lie. Amber had a fuck buddy, not a boyfriend.

"You hesitate!" Ah Ma said.

"No, I did not hesitate."

"Yes, you did. You have a boyfriend! Amber has a boyfriend! This is so exciting! All grandchildren have partners now!"

There was a kerfuffle at the other end of the phone, then Amber's mother said, "You have a boyfriend?"

Amber sighed. "No, I do not."

"Why does your grandmother think you do?"

"I paused for a split second, and she misinterpreted that pause."

"What's his name?"

"Se—I mean, I have no boyfriend!"

Amber was used to lying to her family about her dating life. She carefully controlled the information she gave her parents, grandparents, and three older brothers. No sense making things harder for herself.

But despite all her practice, she'd nearly screwed up just now.

What was wrong with her?

"What did you say?" Mom asked.

"I said I have no boyfriend."

"Okay, I'll take your word for it," Mom said in a completely unconvincing tone.

There was some more banging on the other end of the phone, then Ah Ma was back. "Where did you meet him? At the grocery store? Did you wear sexy clothes?"

God, this was spinning out of control.

Yep, when this conversation was over—Amber had no idea how long it would be—she could use some sex to help her forget.

As it turned out, Sebastian wanted to go out for lunch first. He'd named a wood-oven pizza place downtown that he wanted to try, and Amber's mouth had started watering, even though all her instincts had screamed, "No!"

She loved this restaurant. For half of the year, during the theater festival, it was busy and you needed reservations. It wasn't far from the theaters, and it was popular with the out-of-towners who came to Stratford for a weekend of Shakespeare and other plays.

But at this time of year, they were able to walk right in and get a cozy booth.

It felt like a date. True, lunch was somehow less romantic than dinner, and Sebastian didn't hold her hand under the table, but still. He was wearing a button-down shirt with pale blue stripes, open at the throat, and she couldn't help wanting to climb onto his lap, right here in the booth.

If they had this place all to themselves...

"And for you?"

Oh, shit. The server was here and wanted to know her order. She'd barely looked at the menu, distracted by Sebastian's good looks.

Thankfully, she was familiar with the selections. She ordered the pizza with asiago cheese, three types of mushrooms, and sausage—it was her favorite.

The server left them alone and Amber returned to looking at Sebastian, studying his facial features. He had dark eyes and a slightly wide nose. His jaw was not as square and angular as what she traditionally thought of as ideal masculine features, but somehow, when you put every part of him together, it was perfect.

When she'd seen him at the grocery store, she'd been caught off-guard by his good looks, but now she found him even better looking than she had then.

She nearly reached out to touch his hand, then held herself back.

No, she wouldn't.

This was getting dangerous. It was too much like a relationship. They shouldn't see each other again.

Her heart sank. She'd enjoyed their time together, the bubble tea and the homemade breakfast...

Wait. Why was she focusing on those things? She should be focusing on the sex.

Yes, the sex.

"Has a woman ever grapefruited you?" she blurted out.

His eyebrows drew together. Ooh, he was kind of adorable when he looked puzzled.

*Sexy.* That's what he was. She shouldn't be calling him adorable.

And God, what was wrong with her? Why was she bringing up the weird grapefruit technique? Damn Gloria.

"Here's how it works." She decided that plunging ahead with this conversation was better than any romantic thoughts. "You slice off the sides of the grapefruit and cut a hole in the middle. Big enough for a dick. So for your dick, it would be, um, kind of a big hole, because you're thicker than average. And yes, I've been with lots of guys, so I know these things."

She was trying to put him off her romantically, telling him about this bizarre grapefruit technique, plus the fact that she'd had lots of partners. But of course the latter didn't affect him; he already knew something of her past and had been fine with it.

"Okay," Sebastian said, still frowning. "You put a grapefruit on my dick. Then what?"

"I twist and squeeze the grapefruit around while I suck on the head of your penis."

Sebastian stared at her in wide-eyed horror. "I assure you none of my sexual partners have ever juiced a grapefruit while giving me a blowjob."

"Would you be willing to do it?"

He said nothing.

"I take it that's a no. Oh well, it was worth a try."

He continued to look at her in horror, and then the corners of his mouth twitched and he let out an enormous laugh.

"How do people come up with these things?" he asked.

"I don't know. Apparently it's quite messy—"

"No shit."

"And rather noisy, too. Here, I'll show you the video."

"Amber, I don't want to watch porn in a restaurant."

"It's not porn. She uses a zucchini or cucumber instead...or maybe it's a dildo. Hmm, I forget. I'll show you later. I'm told there's also a scene in *Girls Trip*."

"Well, if you like, we can watch the movie this afternoon."

No! How was this becoming romantic? She was talking about juicing a grapefruit on his dick, and he was talking about watching a movie together. He probably imagined them cuddled up with a bowl of popcorn on her couch.

"How about donuts?" she asked, pushing ahead.

"I like donuts."

"Have you ever used them during sex?"

"I'm not seeing how this would work. Unless you mean the hole..."

"It would go around your dick."

"This is something you've done before?"

She shook her head. "Nah. But would you, if I wanted to?"

He picked up her hand and said, in dramatic fashion, "For you, darling, I'd do anything."

He was goofing around. It was fine. It didn't mean anything.

Though "goofing around" didn't really fit Sebastian's personality—he'd become more comfortable with her in the past few weeks, it seemed.

"I still don't quite know how it works," he said.

"And yet you agreed, without knowing the details."

"Foolish of me, I know."

"I'd just...eat the donut off your dick."

"What kind of donut would you use?" he asked.

"Chocolate dip, I think."

"You answered quickly. You put a lot of thought into it?"

"No, I just like chocolate dip. Though something with sprinkles might be nice."

"Is that so?" He stroked his chin, as though taking this very seriously. "Might be messy."

She imagined multi-colored sprinkles all over his navy sheets. He'd probably hate it.

"Better than Boston cream," she said.

"How would that even work? There's no hole in a Boston cream donut."

"Remember the grapefruit. I could cut a hole in it. You need to be adaptable." She patted his hand again.

"And then there would be cream all over my dick."

"Yeah, I suspect that would be inevitable."

"It would definitely be inevitable," he said. "So after you ate the donut—and hopefully didn't bite me—you'd have to lick off the cream."

"Ooh. Sounds dirty."

"But if you're going to put a donut on my dick," he continued, "you might as well go all-out. Chocolate dip? Boston cream? Those are boring. I used to go to a gourmet donut place in Vancouver, and they had pumpkin spice donuts every fall, filled with pumpkin spice custard."

"Pumpkin spice donut dick. I like it."

"They also had a cherry cheesecake one, with cherry jelly and cheesecake filling."

"OMG, you're making me hungry."

"For donuts?" He waggled his eyebrows. "Or...?"

And even though they'd been talking about something utterly ridiculous, Amber couldn't help clenching her thighs together.

"Both," she said.

"I'd take you to that donut shop if it was anywhere near here."

"There's a donut place in London called Glazed. I went there a few weeks ago."

"We could go together sometime."

He was making plans for the two of them, but Amber couldn't keep doing this. She couldn't go out with Sebastian. Their families would drive them absolutely bonkers, and they already drove her bonkers as it was. She'd only be willing to put up with that if she was head-over-heels in love with him, and she wasn't.

She had to put an end to this. Today would be their last time together. It was getting too intimate for her.

"So, what do you think you'd prefer?" Sebastian asked. "Pumpkin spice donut dick, or cherry cheesecake donut dick?"

"A honey cruller would be less messy, and I think it would flatter the shape of your penis. Though the cherry cheesecake would bring out the color."

"Ahem."

Amber whipped her head around. The server was standing at the end of their table, one pizza in each hand. She told herself not to blush. There was nothing strange about these sorts of conversations at lunch, was there?

Okay, maybe there was.

"Thank you so much," Amber said as the server set down her pizza.

Her dining companion covered his embarrassment by drinking his water.

Unfortunately, he choked.

"You okay?" she asked when the server had walked away.

"I'm fine. But perhaps we should keep the conversation a little more PG-rated for the rest of the meal."

"I know, I'm terrible. You can't take me anywhere."

He smiled at her from across the table, and that definitely did not make her heart sing.

No, it did not.

For dessert, Amber suggested they get tiramisu. To go.

Sebastian looked rather concerned.

"Don't worry," she said. "I'm not going to coat your penis in tiramisu."

"After our earlier conversation, I hope you understand my fears."

"Hmm." She put a finger to her chin and pretended to consider it. "Intriguing idea."

"Amber," he said sternly, in a way that made her want to misbehave.

They did end up getting the tiramisu to go, and when they arrived at Amber's apartment, she slid it onto a plate and placed it on her small dining room table.

"Now let me slip into something more comfortable," she said with a wink.

She went to her bedroom and opened up her night table. She pulled out the skimpy red babydoll that she hadn't worn in quite a while. Normally, she wouldn't put on lingerie for a man who wasn't her boyfriend, but she looked stunning in this, and she wanted Sebastian to see it once.

Because this would be the last time.

There would be no experimenting with grapefruit and donuts in the bedroom. No more swapping pieces of pizza at lunch and clutching the table in laughter.

A tear fell from her eye, and she swiped it away angrily.

She would not cry.

They had no future together, and she was starting to get too attached. This was the way it had to be, and she could handle it like an adult.

She strutted out of the bedroom, chin held high, one hand on her hip.

Sebastian's mouth fell open. He stalked toward Amber, his gaze riveted on her.

"You look...wow."

His mouth collided with hers. One hand came up to squeeze her ass; his other hand was in her hair.

When he slid his lips to her neck, she said, "Don't you want to eat your tiramisu?"

"Later."

"You have something else you'd rather eat?"

"Mm-hmm."

"Well, too bad for you. I want my tiramisu." Admittedly, it would be torture for her as well, but she thought it would be worth it.

"Alright." He led them to the table. "Let's make this fair."

He whipped off his shirt and placed it on the chair next to him.

She swallowed.

He looked particularly good without a shirt. Her eyes lingered on his arm muscles, then followed the light trail of hair...

"We'll eat the tiramisu later," she decided.

"Nope, you wanted to eat it now. So we will."

He held a spoonful of mascarpone cream up to her lips. It was rich and delicious.

It was not the most interesting thing in the room.

"Good girl," he murmured, then had a bite of the dessert himself. He licked his lips slowly, almost obscenely, before feeding her again.

She, in turn, fed him a bite.

"Now keep eating," he said, pulling her into his lap so she was facing the table. As she ate the next few bites of dessert, he slid his hands up and down her bare legs and dipped his fingers inside her barely-there thong, which matched her babydoll. She pressed back against his bare chest.

He hissed out a breath when he touched her wetness.

She was supposed to keep eating, though. So she raised the spoon to her mouth, her hand shaking, and slid it between her lips.

He slipped his finger inside her, and his thumb circled her clit.

She gasped.

"I love the noises you make," he murmured. He continued to stroke her leisurely as she swallowed. "You're so fucking sexy." His other hand rubbed the bottom of her babydoll. "Did you buy this just for me?"

She shook her head. "I've worn it for a bunch of guys."

It was the truth, and she didn't want him to feel special. Because this was all they'd have together.

He plunged two fingers deep inside her, and she shuddered. She rode his fingers, trying to get the right angle, but she couldn't. She groaned in frustration.

"More tiramisu?" He held the spoon to his lips.

"Later. When I can enjoy it properly."

"Why can't you enjoy it properly now?"

"You can be infuriating, you know."

He laughed.

When it was just the two of them, he had a soft, commanding presence. She didn't know how else to describe it. She felt like it was all for her, nobody else was in on this little secret, and she loved it.

He swiped up a small amount of mascarpone cream with his finger and held it to her mouth. She sucked it off, careful to use lots of tongue to drive him wild.

But really. Enough with the tiramisu.

She turned in his lap so she was facing him, her legs wrapped around his waist. The juncture of her legs pressed against his erection, and she groaned again.

How did he feel so good?

How could this be the end?

She unbuttoned his pants and removed his cock through the slit in his boxers, stroking the hard length of him. His size was less intimidating than it had been the first time, but she still required lots of preparation and lube to take him.

He slid his hand into her thong again and worked her into a frenzy. His fingers were no longer enough.

"Sebastian. Please. I need..."

He rolled a condom onto his length, then pulled a small bottle of lube out of his pants—she appreciated that he was prepared.

When he was ready, she raised herself up and pushed her thong to one side. She eased herself down on him, nice and slow, gasping with each additional inch she took of him.

It felt like he was splitting her open, and she would never be able to completely put herself back together.

She didn't care. She kept going.

Finally, his cock was fully inside her.

"Yes, Amber." He sounded in awe of what was happening between them. "You're amazing." He cupped her cheeks and bestowed a single kiss on her lips before shifting his hands to her ass. "Now move."

They thrust together, up and down, in perfect harmony, and she ached. Oh, she ached. This would be it for them.

Why couldn't he be someone else? Someone she hadn't known all her life, someone whose parents were strangers to hers. Someone who wasn't friends with her brother.

*What if...*

No, it was impossible. She couldn't start something real with him unless she was positive it would last. Otherwise, it wasn't worth the risk. She didn't love him.

*But it's already real.*

Amber rode him harder to drown out her thoughts. She kissed him long and deep and held him against her. She took his hand and shoved it into her thong, and he immediately began rubbing her clit.

"Was it like this with anyone else?" he asked as he thrust particularly deep inside her.

She shook her head, unable to be anything but honest when they were together like this.

On and on she rode him. Every inch of her skin sparked with energy, and when her breaths came faster, he pounded into her even harder from below, one hand gripping her thigh, the other moving furiously on her clit.

"Sebastian, I'm going to..."

And then it happened. She shook as though she was breaking into a million pieces, and beneath her, he cried out and tightened his hold on her.

He stayed inside her for a moment, and they simply looked at each other. She felt too raw, though, too naked, and she raised herself up and straightened her clothes.

"Let's finish the tiramisu," she said.

If they were in a real relationship, maybe they could get tested and she could go on the pill. They could stop using condoms; she could feel him go soft inside her.

But none of that would happen.

"Friday is Valentine's Day," he said. "I don't have any plans. Want to come over and spend the evening in bed?"

"Yes," she said before she could stop herself.

She'd sworn this would be the last time, but she couldn't seem to keep away, and she was weak after that incredible orgasm. It was too good with him. They laughed and they ate and they talked and they fucked.

But then she imagined her parents barging into her apartment while she was trying to eat a honey cruller off his dick. An embarrassing situation with any guy, but ten times worse with Sebastian, who knew her family, and it was exactly the sort of thing that would happen to her.

Okay. One more night and then she would end it.

For real this time.

It was Valentine's Day, and Sebastian was nearly ready.

Amber was coming over at eight. As far as she knew, they were going to have sex and order pizza. Cheap pizza, not the thin-crust stuff they'd had the other day.

But he had different plans.

To start, there was a plate of fancy crackers and cheese, as well as wine.

Next, he had a mixed green salad with pear slices and nuts, which he would toss with the balsamic vinaigrette right before they ate.

Then, they would have mussels. He wouldn't cook those until she got here, but everything was ready to go.

For dessert, there was a box of four donuts. Sebastian had driven to London to get them after work. He hadn't known which flavors she'd like, so he'd gotten a selection. He didn't plan on putting one on his dick; he just hoped she'd see the donuts and laugh.

He loved making her laugh.

As soon as she saw everything he'd prepared, she'd know something was up. So before they ate dinner, he planned to tell her the truth. *I'm falling in love with you and I want to have a relationship.*

He wasn't sure what she'd say, to be honest. It was possible she'd walk out before they even got to dinner, but he suspected her feelings toward him had changed, too. Just from the way she'd been with him last weekend, when they went to a cozy restaurant and had sex on a chair afterward, Amber wearing that stunning red slip. It didn't seem like the sort of sex you had with a friend with benefits, even though she hadn't gotten that slip just for him.

There was a knock at the door.

He frowned. It was five minutes to eight, and Amber was never early.

Or maybe she was as excited to see him as he was to see her?

He walked to the door, trying to be all casual and not show his nerves, but when he turned the doorknob and saw who was standing on his porch, his mouth fell open.

It wasn't Amber. It was his parents.

# Chapter 11

*Shit.*

*Shit, shit, shit.*

Fortunately, Sebastian managed not to say any of that out loud. He was thirty years old, but it still seemed wrong to swear in front of his parents.

"Sorry, I have plans," he said to his mom and dad. "I told you to call before you visit."

"What is the point of living so close if we cannot stop in and see you?" Mom said.

"I don't live all that close to Ashton Corners. It's nearly an hour's drive."

*And part of the reason for that was to avoid these situations.*

But apparently he still lived too close to avoid the unexpected drop-in.

"You don't have plans tonight," Mom insisted. "It's Valentine's Day and you don't have a girlfriend. Only couples have plans tonight."

"I have plans," Sebastian repeated. "So you have to go before my visitor arrives."

"Who is your visitor?"

"It's a secret."

Bad call. Now his mother was even more intrigued.

"It must be a girl, don't you think?" she said to his father. "He was lying to us about not having a girlfriend."

Sebastian pinched the bridge of his nose. "I was not lying to you."

"Maybe you are having other single men over?" Mom suggested. "Like a Bro-entine's Day? Let us see what you are preparing."

She ducked under his arm and entered the house.

Sebastian sighed and followed her into the kitchen.

There was a bottle of white wine in an ice bucket. The table was set. There were even candles.

"Looks like a date to me," Dad said. "Your date is a woman, yes?"

Sebastian nodded.

"Ha! You nodded. You agreed you have a date!"

"Yes, I have a date. She's not technically my girlfriend, but we've been seeing each other for a little while. Now, can you please leave? Having my parents here when she arrives would spoil the mood."

"We brought food." Mom lifted up two plastic bags that Sebastian hadn't noticed before. "I need to put it away."

"I'll deal with it," Sebastian said.

"No, I can do it." Mom was already opening up the fridge, and she noticed the box on the counter. "You bought donuts for her! You know, a good chocolate cake would be more romantic. Why donuts?"

Obviously Sebastian wasn't going to mention his conversation with Amber.

He shrugged. "She really likes donuts."

"Tell me more about her. What is her job? Where did she study? Where is she from?"

"She'll be here any minute. Can you please leave?"

He'd been nervous before, and now he was very agitated.

Of course, if everything went well, he'd tell his parents about Amber eventually, but he wasn't ready for that yet—not here, not like this—and without a doubt, she wasn't, either. She'd made her thoughts on family interference clear.

"We're not going anywhere," Mom said as she put a bag of bok choy in the crisper. "I want to meet her. See if she is good enough for you."

"Please, Mom. She's shy. She won't appreciate being ambushed like this. I'll bring her over soon, okay?"

"Hmph."

"Why do you have grapefruit?" Dad asked, holding up the two grapefruit from the fruit bowl on the counter. "I thought you hated grapefruit."

"I changed my mind."

"Or does *she* like grapefruit?" Mom asked. "Grapefruit is breakfast food. You are thinking she will stay overnight? She is not even your girlfriend."

Once again, Sebastian hadn't actually intended to use the grapefruit for any weird sex acts, just as a joke he shared with Amber, but his cheeks flamed.

"Mom." He grasped her hand and started leading her to the front entrance.

Just then, there was a knock on the door.

*Shit, shit, shit.*

"Ah, I am going to meet her!" Mom pulled her hand out of Sebastian's grasp and hurried to the door. She wrenched it open. "Amber, what are you doing here?"

Sebastian's mother was here.

Oh, God, no.

"Hi, Auntie Cecilia. Uncle Randall," Amber said, out of instinct. "Haven't seen you in a while."

She was certain Sebastian hadn't invited his parents over, since he looked as desperate to get out of this situation as she was. His mom and dad must have turned up unexpectedly.

Cecilia glanced between Sebastian and Amber, and then her gaze lingered on Amber. Amber's long coat was undone, and underneath, she was wearing a little black dress and high black boots.

She looked like a woman who planned to have sex tonight.

"What are you wearing, Amber?" Cecilia asked. "That barely counts as a dress. It is a shirt!" She turned to Sebastian. "Amber is your mystery woman. *Amber*?"

"Yes, Mom," Sebastian said, pulling Amber inside. "Now can you please leave?"

"She is the one you are making a romantic dinner for?"

Amber's head snapped toward Sebastian. "What are you talking about?"

"It was supposed to be a surprise," he muttered.

Well, this was certainly a big surprise for Valentine's Day.

It was all wrong. A romantic dinner was the last thing she needed. She'd just wanted to order fast food and fuck one last time.

And now she had to deal with his parents. What terrible luck.

She wanted to sink into the floor.

"Mom, you're making a mess of this," Sebastian said. "Could you leave now so I can talk to Amber alone?"

Cecilia clucked her tongue. "I do not approve of you being with Amber."

"Why not? You're friends with her parents. I thought you'd be thrilled—a little too thrilled."

"Look at her." Cecilia gestured to Amber's barely-there dress. "She is dressed like—"

"Don't say it, Mom!"

It was the first time Amber had ever heard him raise his voice.

"She is not good enough for you," Cecilia went on. "Rosemary and Stuart let her get away with too much. Yes, they are friends, but that doesn't mean I approve of all their parenting methods. Did you know her grandmother caught her buying condoms when she was only seventeen? And she used to give Diana dirty books when they were teenagers."

That had happened a grand total of once.

"You are a doctor," his mother continued. "She went to *Laurier*."

No surprise that Amber's university hadn't been prestigious enough for them.

Amber wanted to talk back, but she couldn't manage it. Cecilia was a family friend, someone she'd been taught to respect.

Randall placed his hand on Cecilia's shoulder. "You have made your point. Let them talk by themselves."

He didn't disagree with anything his wife had said, though.

"Mom." Sebastian's hands were clenched at his sides. "I don't want you to ever, *ever* talk like that." He reached for Amber. "I lo—"

"Nice to see you again!" Amber chirped, waving at his parents.

Sebastian had been about to declare his love for her, hadn't he?

No, she couldn't take it.

Cecilia sniffed, and then she and Randall headed outside. Finally.

Sebastian turned to Amber and wrapped his arms around her. "I'm so sorry. I'll make sure she never says stuff like that again. I promise."

"How would you manage that?"

"Threaten to stop talking to her."

"And you would mean that."

"Yes," he said, "I would."

Admittedly, a part of Amber was thrilled at the firmness in his voice. He was Mr. Perfect Son, but apparently he was willing to throw his parents' approval away for her.

"I told you she didn't like me," Amber said.

"I never heard about the dirty books and the condoms."

"You were away at university."

"It was ten years ago. How can she..." He shook his head. "Listen to me, there is nothing wrong with any of the choices you made. You're perfect just the way you are."

He led her into the kitchen, where the table was set for a nice dinner. There was a vase of roses in the center. Even a tablecloth—she doubted any of her exes knew what a tablecloth was.

He took both her hands in his and looked her in the eye. "I mean it, Amber. When I met you at the grocery store, I thought we'd just have a bit of fun together. I didn't expect to fall for you, but I did. I love your unabashed sexiness, the way you created the life you wanted for yourself, the way you've put yourself out there again and again. I love your cross-stitching and your crochet peacocks and..." He grabbed an envelope off the counter. "Here."

She couldn't stop herself from opening it.

He'd signed them up for the cake class she'd wanted to take in Waterloo.

Some people saw her as the flighty youngest child, but since they'd met again as adults, he'd seemed to appreciate everything about her. It wasn't as if he only liked one part of her or wanted her to be someone other than who she was.

But though she had some rather tender feelings for Sebastian, they were all about friendship and sex. They weren't romantic.

*That's a lie.*

No, it wasn't. She'd been a little worried before about her teeny-tiny feelings of romance, but Sebastian had been about to say he loved her, and she'd recoiled. She definitely didn't love him. That wasn't what she was looking for right now.

Even if she was, going out with him was a terrible idea. Look at what had happened today! His parents had barged their way into his house. What if she'd been eating a donut off his cock? It was fortunate they'd only caught her wearing a revealing dress.

His parents were probably going to have a fight with her parents now.

She wasn't up for this drama. Not for a man she liked but was nowhere close to loving.

"I can't do this," she said to Sebastian, handing back the envelope. "I can't cause problems between you and your parents."

"Don't worry about them. I'll handle it."

"I'm sorry," she whispered. "I don't feel that way about you. I'm so sorry." Tears came to her eyes. He was her friend; she felt badly for not being able to give him what he wanted.

But she couldn't.

He raked a hand through his hair. "I understand. I suppose it's best that we stop seeing each other now.

Just take this before you go." He handed her a box, emblazoned with the logo for Glazed, and she couldn't help the unhinged laugh that came to her lips.

"You bought donuts. For...?"

"No, not for that. Though if you really wanted..." The corner of his mouth kicked up. "I got them to make you laugh, and because you said you like this donut shop."

*Oh, God.*

No, this was all wrong.

She hurried to the door and laced up her impractical boots as quickly as she could.

Sebastian ate the salad by himself. He ate the mussels by himself.

He opened the bottle of wine and drank a large glass before he could even think about what he was doing.

He didn't bother lighting the candles.

He'd told Amber how he felt, and it had been a disaster.

Even if his parents hadn't come at such an awkward time, she said she didn't have those feelings for him.

It wasn't meant to be.

She'd told him she wasn't interested in a relationship, but he'd thought—from the way she kissed him, the way she looked at him—that it had all meant something.

Apparently, he'd been wrong.

He poured himself another glass of wine and sank onto the couch.

# Chapter 12

Amber felt like crap.

Maybe it had something to do with the four donuts she'd eaten in the past twenty-four hours. They'd been delicious, of course: red velvet, carrot cake, crème brûlée, and London fog. She'd never told Sebastian that red velvet was her favorite, but somehow, he'd known to get one.

She hadn't had a good night's sleep, either. Two hours, tops. She'd kept wishing she was lying in bed next to Sebastian. She felt so terribly that she'd broken his heart.

She wished only the best for him.

Amber probably also felt shitty because she'd gotten a dozen texts and calls from her family in the past twenty-four hours, though aside from talking to Ah Ma last night, she hadn't answered any of them.

What had his parents told hers?

*Your wayward daughter is corrupting our precious son!*

Sebastian's parents had arrived in Ashton Corners from Hong Kong when Sebastian was a baby. Upon hearing that there was a new Chinese family in the next town over,

Ah Ma had wanted to visit, and she'd convinced Amber's parents to go with her. Their baby sons had been only three months apart, and they'd become friends. Amber's family had been a bridge, of sorts, between Sebastian's family and their new Canadian small-town life, helping them adjust.

Their families had known each other for decades. And now...

She didn't feel up to dealing with her family yet. Instead, she was having a night out with her friends.

Amber was now tipsy on beer, in addition to being exhausted and high on sugar. She'd also had four cups of coffee earlier, in an attempt to wake herself up. It hadn't worked and probably put her body even more out of whack.

"Anyway," she said, after another gulp of beer, "when his mother basically said I was an underachieving slut, Sebastian was furious."

"Good," Gloria said. "He should have been furious."

"Once they were gone, he told me that I was perfect and he'd fallen in love with me. He had a romantic dinner all planned out." Her voice wavered. "He also signed us up for a cake class."

Roxanne and Gloria looked at each other.

"Why would he do that?" Roxanne asked.

"I told him that I want to take one. I watch baking shows all the time."

"You do?"

"Yeah." Amber paused. "I also crochet little animals as a hobby, but I felt embarrassed telling you two about those things, because you're so talented and I'm..." She gestured vaguely with her hands.

"I knew about the cross-stitching," Gloria said.

"Because I made you an intricate floral piece that said 'Fuck that shit.'"

"Yeah, and I said you should sell them."

"I don't want to turn everything I do into a business, though."

Gloria nodded. "I'm sorry, I didn't get that. But you *are* talented."

"You didn't tell us about baking, but you told Sebastian," Roxanne pointed out.

"I told him a lot of things."

Gloria and Roxanne exchanged looks again. Why did they keep doing that?

"Are you sure you're not in love with him?" Gloria asked. "I haven't seen you this upset in a long time. Like, you and Darren were together for quite a while, and I don't think you were this bothered when you found out he was cheating."

"And all Sebastian has done is treat you well," Roxanne said.

"Yeah, I fall for the losers. I'm broken. I can't fall for the guy who's actually good to me." Amber frowned at her coaster.

"And has a big dick and knows how to use it," Gloria said.

Amber snorted.

"I think you've fallen for him," Roxanne said. "You're just in denial. I'm not sure why. Maybe because of his parents."

"Yesterday was bad enough. I don't want to have to deal with that over and over again. I showed up in an I-want-to-have-sex-tonight dress."

"Think of it this way: you've already reached rock bottom. There's nowhere to go but up. How could it get any worse?"

"If they walked in on me giving him a blowjob and eating a donut off his dick."

"Huh," Gloria said. "Your imagination really is something."

"It's that old sex advice from Cosmo, right?" Roxanne said.

"Yeah, Sebastian and I were laughing about it the other day. You can see how much worse the situation could get."

"With basic precautions—such as locking the door—it seems unlikely something like that would happen. He's willing to take his parents to task for how they acted. Maybe try trusting that he can handle it and will always stick up for you."

"Seems a pity to let this one go when you like him so much," Gloria said. "I agree with Roxanne. You're in deep denial."

"I'm not." Amber knew that wouldn't convince them, though.

Gloria leaned forward. "So tell me. Exactly how big is it?"

Amber's face heated, and then she chuckled at the earnestness in her friend's face. "I'm not telling. That's my secret."

"Fine, fine. Be no fun."

"I'm fun!"

"Yeah, your boyfriend—"

"Sebastian isn't my boyfriend!"

"—is right. You're perfect just the way you are."

Perhaps it was the lack of sleep or the sheer quantity of sugar, caffeine, and booze that had passed through her veins, but Amber hiccupped and shed a few tears.

"You two are great," she said.

"We're also right," Gloria said, giving her a hug. "You'll see. Now I'm curious—do you have any pictures of your crochet animals?"

Amber hadn't planned to go to Sunday dinner at her parents' house that week. But Ah Ma had threatened to drink two piña coladas or drop dead—her threats kept changing—if Amber didn't show up, and she felt guilty. She put on the Hamlet scarf that Ah Yeh had given her and headed out the door.

There were more people at Sunday dinner than usual. Greg, Nick, and their girlfriends had made the drive from Toronto, and everyone was at the door when Amber arrived, twenty minutes late.

"You don't all need to look at me like that," Amber said after taking off her shoes. "I'm perfectly fine."

"I hear you and Sebastian aren't together anymore," Zach said.

"I ended things. It's for the best. I don't feel *that way* about him."

"Are you sure?" Mom asked.

Her family doubted her, just like her friends.

"Do you want me to fight Cecilia and Randall?" Ah Ma lifted up her leg and kicked the air. She lost her balance, and Nick and Greg managed to catch her just in time. "I have mad fighting skills!"

"Sure you do," Dad said.

"You think I am a weak old woman, but I will show you. Hi-yah!" She punched the air with her left fist, then the right.

"Okay, that's enough. You'll hurt yourself."

"Then they will have my death on their conscience. Good! They deserve it. Amber, they said you were not good enough for Sebastian. Wah, they don't know what they are talking about. You are the best girl!"

"Thanks, Ah Ma," Amber said.

"Let me get this straight," Mom said. "You had a sexual relationship with Sebastian, and he wanted it to be romantic, too, but you said no?"

Ugh, Amber wasn't in the mood to hear her mother say "sexual relationship."

"Something like that," she mumbled.

"There's nothing wrong with that. As long as you're enjoying yourself and being treated well, you do what you like." Mom paused. "You haven't had many boyfriends. Is this the sort of thing you do often?"

"I've had many boyfriends, actually," Amber said. "I just haven't told you about most of them. I thought you'd be mad about a few of them, and some didn't last long. I was hoping to avoid your interference in my life. In fact, I've had so many crappy boyfriends that I decided to take a break from dating for a while."

"And then you ran into Sebastian?"

"Yeah."

"Where?"

"At the grocery store." Amber would most certainly not say more than that.

"See? I knew it. The grocery store."

"Could we please not talk about this anymore?"

Dad put his hand on her shoulder. "We want you to know that Cecilia and Randall are wrong. You're definitely good enough for Sebastian. The question is whether he's good enough for you—and that has nothing to do with him being a doctor."

"He definitely is," Amber whispered.

"You know," Zach said, "I like the idea of you two together."

"Me, too," Mom said. "But it's your choice, of course. We won't interfere."

Amber looked around at her family. "You're serious? You won't interfere in my life anymore?"

"Ah, now you are getting carried away," Ah Ma said. "I cannot promise that."

"But I've been thinking," Mom said. "After Zach went so far as to get a fake girlfriend to avoid our matchmaking, and you clearly don't feel comfortable telling us a lot of things…maybe we got a little too involved at times. Besides, relationships aren't for everyone—your aunt Cheryl has been happily single for decades. We shouldn't force it on you. I trust you to make the right decision."

"I've made lots of bad decisions," Amber said.

"And you haven't let that get you down." Mom held out her arms, and Amber embraced her. "We're proud of you, honey, and don't listen to anyone who treats you like you're inferior."

Amber sniffed, a little uncomfortable with the compliments. "I knew Cecilia didn't like me, after the condom incident when I was seventeen."

"We talked about it back then. I told her that you were being safe and I taught you well. She didn't agree, but I had no idea she continued to hold that against you. Until yesterday."

"There was a big fight!" Ah Ma said. "They came over and there was so much yelling. Rosemary even slammed the door on them."

"I didn't mean to cause problems in your friendship," Amber said.

"Don't be sorry about that," Dad said. "They were horrible to you." He gave her a hug.

"I want a hug, too," Ah Ma crashed into the two of them and wrapped her arms around Amber from behind.

Ah Yeh had been silent, and remained so, but he hugged her next, followed by Zach.

Amber released a deep breath. She was lucky to have her family, even if they drove her nuts at times.

Just then, a loud sound pierced her ears.

"Why is the fire alarm going off?" Ah Ma asked.

"It's probably you," Dad said. "This happens almost every time you cook."

"But I haven't touched the kitchen today! I tried, but everyone told me to stay out."

"Oh, shit," Mom said. "I forgot something."

"See? It wasn't my fault!"

Ah Ma and Ah Yeh followed Mom into the kitchen, and Dad removed the battery from the smoke detector.

Zach stayed behind in the front hall with Amber.

"Sebastian is a good guy," Zach said.

"I know," Amber said miserably.

"I never thought I'd fall in love with Jo, and then...well, things changed. Just saying."

Amber was overwhelmed right now. This weekend had been a roller coaster, and she was looking forward to going back to work tomorrow and getting away from it all.

The night at Sebastian's seemed so long ago, but it had only been two days.

And she was starting to wonder...

"I don't know," Amber said. "I'm happy for you, by the way. That your ridiculous fake-relationship plan turned into something real." She thought of Nick and Lily, as well as Greg and Tasha, and a wave of yearning rushed through her.

She might be the Queen of Bad Boyfriends, but she did want to have that one day. She hadn't given up hope; she'd just put it on hold.

Was it possible Sebastian was the guy for her?

Had she really found love in the family planning section of the grocery store pharmacy?

Sebastian had hoped to spend most of the weekend with Amber.

Instead, he spent much of the time going over stuff for work, as well as shopping for things to make his house look more like a home. But what his place could really use was an inappropriate cross-stitch near the front entrance. His parents wouldn't approve, but...

Sebastian liked his life; however, he wondered what would have happened if his parents had never pushed him in any particular direction when it came to his career. If there had been no expectations whatsoever.

Yes, there were things he didn't tell his mom and dad—and he'd refused to move into the house next door—but overall, his life was close to what they wanted for him. Even his long-term relationships had been with women his parents generally approved of.

And then he'd started sleeping with Amber Wong.

He didn't regret anything he'd done or said to them. He would never tolerate such treatment of the woman he loved. He had zero doubts about his feelings for Amber, and for once, he'd done something without a shred of consideration for his parents' expectations.

Amber was entirely his choice. Sure, it had crossed his mind that his parents might be pleased because she was the daughter of their friends, but that hadn't really factored in. Plus, he'd dreaded their meddling.

But he'd been wrong about what his parents would say.

And Amber didn't want him.

He sighed heavily as he sat down at his kitchen table and picked up the envelope with the information for the cake class.

He'd been looking forward to doing that with her, dammit. Everything was fun as long as she was there.

He put on his winter clothes and walked to the grocery store, where he picked up a few things for the week, though he didn't need much. His parents had brought quite a bit of food on Friday.

Then he ventured to the pharmacy section. There was a small selection of greeting cards, and all the Valentine's Day cards were fifty percent off, since the day in question had passed.

He bought one.

He also bought some discounted Valentine's chocolate, remembering all the Christmas chocolate that Amber had had in her basket that day in January.

Sebastian managed a wry smile at that memory.

After returning home and putting away his groceries, he jumped in his car and headed to his parents' house. He'd promised he'd come over for dinner today, and he wasn't particularly looking forward to it.

"I won't let you speak to Amber like that ever again," Sebastian said.

"Is she your girlfriend now?" his mother asked.

They were sitting around the kitchen table in his childhood home: Sebastian, his mother, and his father.

"No," Sebastian said, "but if you see her again, you better not act like that."

"We had a fight with Rosemary and Stuart," Mom said.

"They stuck up for their daughter? Good."

Mom crossed her arms and looked at him as though trying to figure him out. Perhaps she thought this was out of character for him—he'd never been the rebellious child.

"You were okay with them setting up Diana and Zach," he said. "But for me and Amber, it's different?"

Was it because they considered Zach more respectable...and they'd never seen Zach wearing a short *I'm-here-to-have-sex* dress? Or because they had more specific expectations for Sebastian than Diana?

Not that it mattered.

Dad finally opened his mouth. "You really love her."

"Yeah. I do."

*I've never quite felt this way before.*

"Then if you bring her home, I will welcome her. We will try to be more open-minded. She is not who we imagined for you, but maybe she is right for you." He gave Sebastian a small smile.

Sebastian exhaled. If he'd won over his dad, then his dad would eventually convince his mother. "One other thing. Boundaries. Please don't show up unannounced and force your way in when I say no, okay? I'll try to visit you every week now that I'm close by, but at the very least, call before you get in the car."

"That is fine, Sebastian," Dad said. "We understand."

Mom didn't seem thrilled, but she nodded.

He knew his parents wanted the best for him. They'd come to this country for opportunities, to give their children a better life, but they had specific ideas of what that meant, and they were a little rigid in their thinking.

They would figure this out, though.

He felt a heaviness in his heart as he thought of Amber. He wanted her to be an important part of his life, but he'd already put his heart out there and been rejected.

Perhaps she'd come to him later, after she got his package in the mail.

Perhaps not, but it was her choice, and he'd let her make it on her own.

"I'm thankful for what you've done for me," he said to his parents, "but I have my own life now and I can decide what's best for me." He paused. "I love you."

His parents looked at each other like they didn't know what to make of his words, then turned back to him.

"Ah, I almost forgot," Dad said. "There was a big sale this weekend on paper towels. They're in the basement. I will get them for you."

"We went to London and got the bao you like," Mom said, heading to the fridge. "And those chocolate cookies—they are so hard to find."

Though they didn't say the words, this was how they told Sebastian that they loved him.

# Chapter 13

When Amber came home on Monday after work, she took down the sign that had hung above her bed for a year.

*Rule #1: No Dating.*

After having leftovers for dinner—her parents had sent food home with her yesterday—she sat in front of the TV, ready to crochet and watch some baking shows. She'd bought a pattern for an otter holding a heart, and she was excited to get started.

The truth was, there was a purpose to the otter. And her next crochet project, which made her giggle stupidly.

She was making them all for Sebastian. A plan had formed at the back of her mind, and she was slowly putting it into action.

As she worked on her little projects, she allowed the feelings she'd ignored for so long to bubble to the surface. She'd been so resistant to the idea of them being together, but after talking to her friends and her family, she'd been slowly changing her mind.

She didn't suddenly know in a flash that she wanted to be with him for always, but that didn't mean it was any less. She'd been impulsive in the past. Now, she was taking her time.

For some reason, she needed this time alone, and she let herself have it.

The following Wednesday, she received a small package. She got a goofy grin on her face when she saw that it was from Sebastian, and she immediately tore it open.

There was a bag of chocolate hearts with a "50% off" sticker. She was sure he'd left the sticker on deliberately.

There was also an envelope sealed with a heart. Inside, she found a card with two heart balloons and the words "Be Mine." When she opened it up, a piece of paper fluttered out.

It was the registration for the cake class. He'd added a sticky note saying he could change the name of the second person so she could take it with a friend.

In the card, he'd written, *If you change your mind, I'm here. Love, Sebastian.*

The next move was on her. She didn't expect to hear from him again otherwise—he would give her space. She appreciated that, but at the same time, she wanted to run to him and throw her arms around him.

But she would wait a little longer.

Until her plans were in order.

Until she was absolutely sure.

Screw that.

She was absolutely sure now. She wanted to be with him more than anything. And unlike many of the men she'd dated in the past, he was kind and thoughtful and he made her feel good about who she was.

There was still the issue of their families, but Roxanne was right when she said the worst thing that could happen had already happened. Yes, it might be annoying at times, but it was worth it. Amber wouldn't give this up just because there were some issues. She could stand up for herself when she needed to, and Sebastian would be on her side; she knew she could count on him.

All of a sudden, she ached, absolutely ached, to have his arms around her once more.

She sent him a text.

Sebastian figured it was a good sign that Amber had invited him over that Friday.

Still, he didn't expect the sight that greeted him when he opened the door.

Well, he'd expected Amber, looking lovely, of course. She was wearing the same dress she'd worn on Valentine's Day. For a moment, he could look nowhere but at her.

But then he noticed the red and pink streamers. The heart-shaped balloons.

That was a surprise.

"I'm sorry about Valentine's Day." Her voice, normally strong, wavered. He squeezed her hand. "I was caught off-guard. But that doesn't mean I hadn't already been falling for you. I had—but I kept it a secret, even from myself. I can be a little dim sometimes."

He shook his head. "No, you are a bright light, and my life is so much better for having you in it."

"When you pulled a box of Magnum condoms off the shelf, I never would have imagined you saying something like that to me one day." She took a deep breath, and he couldn't stop smiling at her. "I didn't plan on it being more than sex—and the sex was amazing, even if we, uh, had trouble making it work the first time. But then we began hanging out, outside of the bedroom. I told you things that I don't usually tell other people. We spent nights together. You made me breakfast. It was..." She shut her eyes for a moment. "It was better than any relationship I'd had. It was finally the relationship I deserved—because I deserve better than what all those assholes gave me. I just wasn't looking for it with you, so I couldn't see it. But now, I'm looking, and I love you. I love the way I feel when I'm with you."

"Me, too," he said quietly.

He'd been missing something in his life. Someone he could relax around, someone he could have fun with.

But she was so much more than that to him.

He didn't have the words, though, so he pulled her into his arms and kissed her. Unlike the first time, it wasn't a kiss that came simply from lust, but one with a deeper passion, an emotional bond.

It felt so good to have her body pressed up against his again. To have her in his arms, feeling like they were both where they belonged.

When he began kissing down the side of her neck, she stepped back. "Before we get carried away, I want the chance to do Valentine's Day over again." She led him into the living room, where there were three packages wrapped in red and pink paper, and handed him one. "Open this first."

It was a pair of crochet otters, each holding a red heart.

"You made these," he said.

"Just for you."

"They're adorable."

She handed him the next package.

This one rendered him speechless. It was another crochet project, but it wasn't what he'd call *adorable*.

It was a crochet penis.

Yes, she'd made him a light brown penis. With balls, of course.

"It's very...phallic." He was unsure what else to say.

"It's meant to be to scale," she said. "Want to check?"

"Soon, I promise."

The next present was a crochet donut with pink frosting. Which, by itself, was rather cute, but he knew what she intended him to do with it.

God, he loved this woman.

He slid the donut on top of the crochet dick. It was a perfect fit.

He swallowed. "About our families..."

"We'll do our best to ensure they don't interfere too much. My mom admitted they get a bit too involved at times."

"And my parents understand that I love you and won't tolerate them talking that way. In time, they'll come to like you—I can't see how they wouldn't. But we'll figure it out together."

She nodded. "I have something else for you, too."

"You've already given me so much."

"I know, a Magnum-size crochet dick really put it over the top. Though that was a little more successful than what I'm about to show you."

She led him to the kitchen, where there was a plate of cupcakes on the counter. They had white icing and red heart candies, but they didn't look like the sort of thing that could be sold in a bakery. Rather, they looked like something that might appear on *Nailed It!*

He'd binge-watched baking shows in the past week. It had made him feel closer to her.

"As you can see," she said, "I definitely need some classes. Will you take them with me?"

"Absolutely." He smiled.

"Now, although these don't look gorgeous, they taste all right." She put a lopsided cupcake on a plate. "Red velvet with cream cheese buttercream. It was my first time making buttercream, and it's a little grainy, but…" She swiped some buttercream off the cupcake and held it to his lips.

"Mm. That's good."

She swiped up more buttercream and put it just above the low neckline of her black dress. "Want a taste?"

"Oh, do I ever. But I can't help worrying that your dress is going to get dirty."

He pushed the thin straps off her arms and unzipped the dress. She shimmied out of it.

"The bra will have to go, too." He unclasped her strapless bra and tossed it on the floor.

Now she stood before him, wearing only black lacy panties and a bite of cream cheese buttercream. She looked utterly delectable.

"Happy Valentine's Day," he murmured.

Then he licked off the buttercream and carried her to bed.

# Epilogue

"Dammit, it doesn't fit!"

Amber tried, once again, to slide the chocolate dip donut with sprinkles onto her boyfriend's dick. One side of the donut split to accommodate Sebastian's girth, even though she'd selected the donut with the largest hole.

"I think that's a sign it wasn't meant to be." Sebastian stroked her hair. "I'm a little relieved, to be honest. I was worried you might accidentally bite in the wrong place."

"I would have been very careful, I assure you," Amber said, pretending to be offended by Sebastian's lack of faith in her eating-donut-off-dick abilities.

In general, he had lots of faith in her, but not here.

She tore the donut in two and handed one half to Sebastian. After they'd consumed the donut, she gave him a blowjob without any donuts or grapefruit.

That was how they spent the morning of Easter Sunday: in bed.

But at eleven o'clock, they had to get dressed in proper clothes—rather than the skimpy red lingerie Amber had been wearing for the past hour—and head to Mosquito Bay.

That was okay. Amber had had lots of time alone with Sebastian lately.

They'd officially been together for over a month, and it was, without a doubt, the best relationship she'd ever had, and she couldn't imagine it being any better than this. They went out for bubble tea together. They baked together—with limited success, but they were improving. They went grocery shopping together. They lay in bed and snuggled. They laughed a lot. Occasionally, they went out for drinks at The Tempest with her friends.

The best part was simply getting to be with him all the time, this wonderful man who loved her just the way she was.

Though Amber's family wasn't religious, they celebrated Easter with a ham lunch, which her mother prepared. There would also be noodles—Ah Yeh's noodles appeared at every family holiday—scalloped potatoes, salad, and lots of other food. Perhaps Lily and Nick would bring Nanaimo bars.

Given that all the Wong children now had significant others, this Easter lunch would be more crowded than usual. Sebastian's family would be coming this year as well.

An hour after leaving Mosquito Bay, Amber arrived at the brick house where she'd grown up. She and Sebastian walked up the flagstone path hand in hand, and before Amber could ring the doorbell, the door opened.

"Hello!" Ah Ma said. "Happy Easter!" She held up the colorful drink in her hand, garnished with a pink umbrella.

"Ah Ma, it's noon," Amber said. "Have you already started drinking?"

"These are virgin piña coladas, don't worry. Very healthy."

"Um, I'm not sure piña coladas are healthy, even without the booze."

"Who cares? I am old. I will do whatever I like!"

Just then, a six-foot-tall pink Easter Bunny walked into the front hall. He was carrying a basket of chocolate eggs and wearing a grumpy expression.

"Greg, you are supposed to smile." Ah Ma pinched his cheek, which she was barely able to reach.

"Why is my brother dressed as the Easter Bunny?" Amber asked.

"Ah Yeh ordered the costume on Amazon," Greg said with a sigh. "We took a vote, and everyone thought I should wear it. Personally, I voted for Nick."

Tasha bounded into the hall. "I think he looks cute."

Amber plucked a chocolate egg out of Greg's basket and passed it to Sebastian. She took a second one for herself.

"Hey, Amber." Zach walked into the hall, holding Jo's hand. "How was the drive?"

"Not too bad. We didn't get stuck in a snowstorm and spend the night in an unheated motel room, so I can't complain."

"It's April," Greg pointed out. "A snowstorm is unlikely."

"You never know," Ah Ma said. "I am powerful! I can control the weather. But now there is no need for matchmaking, because you have all been matched, thanks to me."

"Um," Nick said. "You guys set Lily up with Greg, not me."

"And you set Zach up with Sebastian's sister," Amber said, "rather than setting me up with Sebastian."

Ah Ma tapped her finger against her chin. "I have secrets."

"Before I forget." Amber pulled a package out of her purse and handed it to Jo. "This is for you."

Jo unwrapped the green paper.

"You made this, Amber?" Ah Ma said. "I don't understand. It looks like a banana."

"I don't think it's a banana," Jo said. "It looks more like a penis."

"Just like the shaft you drew at Chinese New Year, the last time I saw you," Amber said. "I'm looking forward to playing Pictionary against you next year, with my new teammate." She squeezed Sebastian's hand, and he squeezed back.

The doorbell rang, and Amber opened the door, revealing Sebastian's parents and sister.

"You are here!" Ah Ma said. "Just in time. Look what Amber made for Jo." She pulled Jo's gift out of her hand and held it up in the air.

Amber put her hands over her face and shook her head. Things had been going reasonably well with Sebastian's parents, but she hadn't needed them to see that.

Cecilia and Randall exchanged slightly horrified glances, but then Cecilia said, "You are very, ah, talented, Amber."

Huh. Her future mother-in-law was complimenting her crochet dick.

Yes, she expected Cecilia would be her mother-in-law one day. She couldn't imagine marrying any man but Sebastian.

"Isn't it awesome?" Ah Ma said, and her enthusiasm over the crochet dick made Amber wonder if those really were virgin piña coladas.

Ah Ma led the way into the kitchen, where Mom was absently stirring a pot on the stove as she kissed Dad.

"Okay, Mom and Dad," Nick said. "Time to break it up."

"You're all here!" Mom said. "Happy Easter, everyone! I'm especially pleased that the Easter Bunny was able to join us this year."

Everyone looked in Greg's direction and clapped.

"Can I take this costume off yet?" Greg muttered.

Amber laughed and leaned back against Sebastian, who wrapped his arms around her.

She was with her family and the man she loved for the holidays, and there was nowhere else she'd rather be. And when she got home that night, she'd give Sebastian the cross-stitch she'd made for him.

It said: *Amber Wong has the world's best boyfriend.*

# About the Author

Jackie Lau decided she wanted to be a writer when she was in grade two, sometime between writing "The Heart That Got Lost" and "The Land of Shapes." She later studied engineering and worked as a geophysicist before turning to writing romance novels. Jackie lives in Toronto with her husband, and despite living in Canada her whole life, she hates winter. When she's not writing, she enjoys gelato, gourmet donuts, cooking, hiking, and reading on the balcony when it's raining.

To learn more and sign up for her newsletter,
visit jackielaubooks.com.

# Also by Jackie Lau

*Love, Lies, and Cherry Pie*

**Donut Fall in Love Series**
*Donut Fall in Love*
*The Stand-Up Groomsman*

**Weddings with the Moks Series**
*Four Weddings to Fall in Love*
*Three Reasons to Run*

**Chu's Restaurant Series**
*The Sitcom Star*
*The Reluctant Heartthrob*

**Kwan Sisters/Fong Brothers Series**
*Grumpy Fake Boyfriend*
*Mr. Hotshot CEO*
*Pregnant by the Playboy*
*Bidding for the Bachelor*


**Cider Bar Sisters Series**
*Her Big City Neighbor*
*His Grumpy Childhood Friend*
*Her Pretend Christmas Date* (novella)
*The Professor Next Door*
*Her Favorite Rebound*
*Her Unexpected Roommate*


**Holidays with the Wongs Series**
*A Match Made for Thanksgiving*
*A Second Chance Road Trip for Christmas*
*A Fake Girlfriend for Chinese New Year*
*A Big Surprise for Valentine's Day*

**Baldwin Village Series**

*One Bed for Christmas* (prequel novella)

*The Ultimate Pi Day Party*

*Ice Cream Lover*

*Man vs. Durian*


**Chin-Williams Series**

*Not Another Family Wedding*

*He's Not My Boyfriend*